PROJECT TISIPHONE

THE LONG RUN
BOOK 3

LEAH R CUTTER

KNOTTED ROAD PRESS

ALSO BY LEAH R CUTTER

Science Fiction

The Long Run

Project Nemesis

Project Nyx

Project Tisiphone

Project Persephone

War of the Allied Worlds

The Labors of Darius Linard

Huli Intergalactic: Science/Space Fantasy

Origins

The Strawberry Girl

Urban/Contemporary Fantasy Series

The Cassie Stories

Poisoned Pearls

Tainted Waters

Spoiled Harvest

Bloodied Ice

The Witch's Progress

Circle of Air

Circle of Fire

Circle of Water

Circle of Earth

Seattle Trolls

The Changeling Troll

The Princess Troll

The Fairy-Bridge Troll

The Troll-Demon War

The Troll-Human War

The Troll-Troll War

The Shadow Wars Trilogy

The Raven and the Dancing Tiger

The Guardian Hound

War Among the Crocodiles

The Clockwork Fairy Kingdom

The Clockwork Fairy Kingdom

The Maker, the Teacher, and the Monster

The Dwarven Wars

The Chronicles of Franklin

Franklin Versus The Popcorn Thief

Franklin Versus The Soul Thief

Franklin Versus The Child Thief

Epic Fantasy Series

Houses of the Dead

Houses Divided

Houses Fallen

Houses Reborn

Forgotten Gods

A Wind Blown Torment

A Stone Strewn Clash

A Sea Washed Victory

The Tanesh Empire Trilogy

The Glass Magician

The Desert Heart

The Ghost Dog

Mysteries

The Purloined Letter Opener

The Tell Tale Heart Pin

Dancer in Darkness

Trophy Hunters

The Alvin Goodfellow Case Files

The Rabbit Mysteries

The Shredded Veil Mysteries

Mystery, Crime, and Mayhem

CHAPTER 1
FREDRICK

What a pissy little Human.

Of course, Fredrick didn't say any of what he was thinking out loud. Just as he didn't allow it to show on his black face, or in his blue-gray eyes. His white fur just laid there, the hackles not rising no matter how this Human, Clayton, might snip at him.

Fredrick was the consummate professional, despite his Yu'udir nature. Or perhaps, in part, because of it.

He kept his black claws trimmed short, though never blunted. He'd also learned to eat more like a Human instead of tearing apart his meat with his sharp teeth. In addition, he had tricks like bending his knees slightly so that he didn't tower so far over everyone. He worked at compressing his presence, making it easier to overlook him.

His patience, and his hard work, were finally paying off. He didn't allow himself to think about all the times he'd bowed and scraped to get by, allowing someone else to appear to have had the brilliant idea instead of insisting on credit himself.

All of that had put him on the path to this moment, so

that he could be in this position, promoted several steps above his previous superiors, finally in charge of a serious operation.

Something the silly Human called *Project Tisiphone*, based on an old legend of an avenging goddess.

This was Fredrick's chance to prove himself, to prove that he wasn't the brute his ex-wife claimed he was. Nor the coward his other ex-wife had ridiculed him as.

Fredrick found it interesting that he was to report directly to Clayton, one of the movers and shakers on the board of directors for The Universal Trading Cartel. "Universal" as it was known by those who worked for it, "the Cartel" for all those on the outside.

Those little people who didn't know any better.

Reporting directly to Clayton had both its advantages as well as disadvantages. It meant that no one would see his work and that his new boss could claim all the credit. Fredrick understood that he was working far, far off the beaten track, on a whole different set of books. Ones that no one would ever admit the existence of.

However, if Fredrick did well, it meant that he would have access to an entirely new collection of powerful people. He could parlay that into an even better position. Though he doubted that any of them would be less pissy than the little Human seated in front of him.

At least Clayton appeared to have some level of vision, despite how much of a pissant he appeared to be. He'd been chasing ghosts, as it were. Ships that had been registered to Arthur, the most famous Yu'udir of all.

Ships that were now, suddenly, weeks and months after the space station *Camelot* had been blown up, using their credentials for the first time.

Fredrick had been the one who had put together the "coincidences" that had occurred in Gamor, a Bantel system.

A single mishap wouldn't necessarily have triggered any alarms.

But there had been more than one. One of Arthur's ghost ships had shown up at the space station, a "special" ship had been offered as a bribe to some less-than-honest Universal employees, and before that female Bantel could be brought in for further questioning, an emergency had occurred at the station, some sort of hull breach, enabling her to leave the station and the paperwork associated with her transfer conveniently lost.

Too many strange occurrences in too short of a period of time.

It was the sort of data analysis that only a thinking person could do. A machine couldn't be trained to catch such a thing. It required too much intuition, and no way to program in "this is different" whereas "this isn't."

Fredrick had known that he was taking a chance bringing his findings to the attention of Clayton (though at the time he'd just raised the flags and hoped that someone up above him was actually paying attention).

The gamble had been worth it.

Now, he'd moved to the Armadillo system, onto the *Dallas* space station itself, meeting with Clayton.

The Human's office left much to be desired. It was supposed to look rugged, Fredrick supposed, what with the arid landscape being portrayed on the holograms covering the walls, the horns of a herd animal (those long points were obviously defensive, not offensive) and some sort of leather contraption that Humans sat on (again, on herd animals, nothing wild).

Frederick wore a somber forest-green vest with the cooling element it encased cranked to its highest setting. He wished he could have worn his matching flat cap as well, with its cooling ice gel inside, but he'd known that Clayton would have taken offense.

This soft Human who wouldn't have lasted a day on the ice floes of Fredrick's home world, to say nothing of the plains he clearly admired.

The man before him was all teeth and no bones, as the Yu'udir might say—able to tear his meat apart, but without any souvenirs from his own personal kills.

And yet—had Clayton had a hand in the destruction of *Camelot*? Fredrick wasn't certain. The lines were still too blurry, the ink and the blood too fresh.

If this Human had anything to do with the tragedy, anything at all, he shouldn't have any trophies. Even being on the board of Universal wouldn't protect him. The board would collectively turn their backs on him, eagerly dividing up his shares among those considered more worthy, all the while claiming they had nothing to do with it.

Which they may or may not have.

Fredrick was eager to start his work, to see what he could find in Clayton's system, if there was a way to pin the killing of *Camelot* on his new boss.

What sort of proof could he find? And what did he want to do, if he found it?

Blackmail was trickier than walking across a melting lake. One wrong footstep and you'd drown. However, Clayton certainly had enough credits to fund even the most extravagant of Fredrick's dreams.

Maybe he wasn't dreaming big enough.

Or, instead, did he want to find the proof of Clayton's deeds and turn him in? Fredrick would be hailed as a hero among his people. If he did that, and played his cards perfectly, perhaps, maybe, he would be granted Clayton's shares of stock as part of his reward.

Decisions, decisions.

Nothing to do about it today though, except to worm his way completely into Clayton's organization. He still didn't know the truth. It would be a while, and a lot of careful digging, before he did.

"Do you have any questions?" Clayton said finally after he'd stopped pontificating and appeared to notice that Fredrick wasn't hanging on his every word.

"No, sir," Fredrick said, keeping his tone soft and polite. "I will get right on it. And report to you immediately the moment I find something."

"Good," Clayton said. "And you understand the need for secrecy, as well."

"I do," Fredrick said, nodding. "Can't have the riff-raff sniffing around, casting blame where it shouldn't be."

"And where should it be placed?" Clayton asked. He sounded friendly enough, but Fredrick already had a good read on this Human.

"Why, on Arthur, of course!" Fredrick said. "We all know that he was working on some experimental projects on *Camelot*. One of those must have had a critical malfunction, exploded at just the wrong time, in the wrong place, that set off an unfortunate chain reaction. And that happened at a once-in-a-lifetime concurrence of events, just as some minor space debris slammed into the station."

Fredrick maintained his soft, British-English professorial tone throughout his speculation.

"Yes! Exactly," Clayton said, beaming at Fredrick. "You see why it's absurd to believe that any one person might have been successful at such a cataclysmic event."

"The Khanvassa would say that it was ordained by their Goddess, for such a thing to occur," Fredrick added.

"And what do you think actually happened?" Clayton asked. He sounded unconcerned, even looking away from Fredrick to hide his eyes.

"I have no idea," Fredrick proclaimed. "Except that Arthur might have gotten what was coming to him."

"I'm surprised you feel that way," Clayton said, honest puzzlement in his face, though his eyes were still masked. "Being Yu'udir and all."

"Please," Fredrick said. "We are not ignorant. We must work together, or we will all starve. A lone person on the ice is a dead person." He paused, then caught Clayton's eye and held it. "And Arthur was working alone."

"You understand," Clayton said after a few moments. "Good. I am looking forward to working with you."

"And I, you, sir," Fredrick said. He stood, understanding the dismissal for what it was. "I will start my search immediately."

"Work with my secretary to get whatever access you need," Clayton said. "You must find these ghosts. Figure out why they're appearing. See if there's some remnant of *Camelot* that needs to be purged."

"You can count on me," Fredrick said, nodding, then heading out the door.

Oh, yes. Clayton had been involved in the destruction of *Camelot*.

And sooner or later, Fredrick would find the proof he needed, to the detriment of this pissant Human. While at the same time, enriching his own world.

CHAPTER 2

JUDIT

Judit wasn't sure exactly what to do, or who to blame, for their most recent luck.

Eleanor and her crew had just successfully completed three cargo runs. There was actually a trickle of money flowing *into* her personal accounts again, instead of it all flowing *out*.

Something would be going terribly wrong soon.

"Would you at least consider not grinding your teeth so hard?" Saxon complained. He sat beside her in the main helm of the spaceship *Eleanor*. "I mean, it isn't as if you have points or something to shave off." He gave her a particularly toothy grin, showing his own sharp teeth, white against the completely black face of a Yu'udir. The blue vest he wore that day made his own blue eyes look searing, and the gold pilot's couch he laid on really highlighted all his white fur.

"*Baszd meg,*" Judit replied. Softly.

Okay, so not softly enough, give the single eyebrow that Saxon raised in her direction.

"I can't help it," Judit said, indicating the normal looking space station they were rapidly approaching. It was a modern station, with rings that went up and down, instead of one of the older stations that "just growed" and had compartments and docks attached at random.

The space station *Balmor* was primarily Human. Judit and Saxon had been there before, and she knew that it had large sections dedicated to each of the alien species that made up Cartel space. There was even a small section for the Chonchu, the most reclusive of all the aliens, who, according to Eleanor, were basically trapped in their home system by the Cartel.

While Judit had worked at finding cargo to ship to space stations and areas that weren't as controlled by the Cartel, she couldn't completely avoid them. The Gamor system that they'd been at, that they'd had to break Kim out of, had had a large Cartel presence. Many of the Bantel systems now did, as evidently they'd tried something like a coup way back in the day.

The *Balmor* space station didn't have a large number of Cartel personnel on it. Nor was it a small percentage. Merely about average, as far as Basil could tell.

"Why can't you help grinding your teeth so uselessly?" Saxon prompted as he fiddled a bit with the controls, adjusting their exact course into the space station.

"We've just—it's just been good for a while, you know?" Judit said. She felt stupid saying anything out loud. But Saxon was a friend, really the only friend she had left from the old days. She'd left the tiny space station she'd grown up on decades before when she'd signed on with Miklós, a local trader who'd treated her like a granddaughter. When he'd retired, she'd purchased the trading ship from him, and Saxon had been one of the few members of the crew who had stayed with her.

"It has been good for the last few runs," Saxon said. "So,

I suppose that means, according to your twisted logic, that we're due for some bad luck?"

"You got it," Judit said, nodding grimly. "And it will be awful, to make up for all the good things that have happened recently." Like Basil, her engineering nerd and Oligochuno, finally figuring out exactly the right formula that the secondary engines used for cooling. Zie'd even managed to tweak it slightly, to increase its life expectancy.

Or like the Bantel Kim, the nominal communications expert for the ship. She'd been working extra hard to prove that she was one of them, one *with* them, at least until they had enough money to live on their own. She'd found the station chatter about the "special ship" and had traced the call back to one of the Cartel headquarters, in the *Dallas* system.

So Judit and the crew knew that not only was someone looking for them, whoever it was held a high position in the Cartel.

Hell, even Judit had had some good luck, finding the cargo they were currently shipping. It was a short run, from one system to the next using the standard hyperspace tunnels. But the client had paid extra (a lot extra) for the specialized shipping compartments that *Eleanor* had, as well as a bonus for speedy delivery.

Judit had an ace up her sleeve in that regard. *Eleanor* had been an experimental ship, built by Arthur the Yu'udir, on his space station *Camelot*, before it had been destroyed by the Cartel. She didn't have to use the existing hyperspace tunnels, but could dig her own.

And digging her own tunnels meant she was a *lot* faster than anyone else.

Menefry, her Khanvassa security technician, had cause to believe that he might find some (relatively) inexpensive cloaking apparatus here in the *Balmor* station.

They needed it. If they could leave a space station, then disappear before reaching the regular hyperspace tunnels, and instead, dig their own out of any system, that would make them a lot less traceable.

The Cartel had guards at every hyperspace gate that left a system. They kept track of every ship that went through. It was why they'd been running through all the various ship registrations that they had access to, though this time, they'd end up having to repeat, and use the first one again.

"Could it be that this run of good luck is just compensating for the incredible bad luck we'd had previously?" Saxon asked innocently.

Well, he tried for innocent. Missed it by a good light year.

"What bad luck?" Judit asked.

"Oh, let's see. Being turned in by one of our own crew members, set up on charges of smuggling," Saxon said, ticking the items off one by one on his black claws. "Working with Arthur, only to have the entire space station *Camelot* blow up."

He paused for a moment, his eyes turning bleak.

"Hey, it's okay," Judit said, reaching out and patting his soft furry arm.

The death of *Camelot* and the dream it had represented to the Yu'udir had hit Saxon hardest of all the crew. He had the most rage of all of them at the untimely deaths of everyone who'd been on that station, sacrificed by the Cartel.

Saxon shook his head and peered out at Judit again, instead of that ice-filled wrathful place he'd been in. "Sorry," he said.

"I wouldn't count *Camelot* as just a little bad luck," Judit told him gently.

Saxon nodded.

"However, I still feel as though we have some bad luck

coming our way," Judit said, turning back to study the *Balmor* station that was rapidly growing on the front screens.

It was something that she truly appreciated about *Eleanor*. In her own perfect world, the front windows of the main helm would be a touch bigger. Not much. Just a touch. They already went all the way from one side of the small helm to the other, and from the console up along the curve of the ship.

The pilot's couch was incredibly comfortable, and the right combination of support and softness. The gold color wasn't exactly to her taste, but she'd grown used to it. The walls were tinted green and silver, instead of some drab industrial gray, and the black rubber floors had a nice sheen to them that reflected the light instead of absorbing it all.

While Judit could perform her duties at a more reclined angle, she tended to sit up and just be webbed in, in case the gravity suddenly went out.

Stranger things had happened on *Eleanor*, which was why Judit was always strapped in.

The space station they were approaching was big enough to have actual docking bays. This meant that Judit would pilot *Eleanor* directly into the station itself, instead of attaching to the side of it.

Basil was particularly excited about this, hoping to get additional work done on *Eleanor* while they were in the equivalent of a dry dock.

Judit wasn't sure how much she would allow zim to work on the exterior of the ship.

Eleanor was *special*, with a secondary engine system unlike anything else in the galaxy right now.

And they needed to make sure that no one looked at them too hard or for too long.

Basil had promised to be careful, going so far as to work with Kim on some camouflaging fabric that would hide zim.

It was just one of the many ways in which Judit could see their luck finally running out.

"We'll all be careful while we're here," Saxon assured Judit.

She shook her head but didn't say anything.

Careful had nothing to do with it.

Eventually, their luck would just run out.

And they'd be on the run again.

Or worse.

CHAPTER 3
MENEFRY

MENEFRY LAY FLAT ON HIS BACK, THE MOST VULNERABLE position for the Khanvassa. He prayed in that position, to make himself more open to the Goddess Nesnefera, may her eight-limbs always be raised in joy. His cabin on *Eleanor* had been specially built for him, which was something he appreciated more and more as he continued his journey with this crew.

In addition to the walls being plain, with no supposed artwork hanging on them (as that was an insult to the Goddess), all the doorways were taller and wider to fit his extra height and bulk. He had a front room in which he could entertain other people if he so chose. He'd purchased an additional statue of the Goddess for that room, one with all of her arms spread wide in welcome.

There were pillows in neutral colors that he could use to recline upon, as well as additional blankets, all white of course. He kept the temperature in his rooms much warmer than the rest of the ship, just so he could relax. However, some nights it was better to swaddle himself, wrapping himself up tightly, so he could be extra warm in his cocoon.

In his sleeping room, he kept the statue of the Goddess in Flux, her arms waving all around her, one foot raised as if about to take a step. She was painted the traditional black, with a waft of golden fabric draped over her figure.

Menefry had carefully placed the Goddess in his room on the cupboard next to the door. As part of the thoughtful build of his room, there was a niche cut out of the wall which was the perfect size for him to lie down in and pray.

The statue could look down on him while he did, and he could gaze upon the Goddess as well.

When he'd first gotten the statue, he'd placed the red ribbons she'd been wrapped in into her hands, the idea being that if the ribbons fell, the Goddess was unhappy about where she'd been put and he would have to find a different location for her.

Fortunately, she'd seemed happy enough in her current location, though Menefry had adjusted her a few times, just so he could see her face better.

Except—the expression on this manifestation of the Goddess always puzzled him. She appeared to be content in her state of flux. Or was she just meditating on the state of change?

Menefry was himself still in flux, in between things. Part of the problem was that he wasn't certain what he was between. He knew his past, had spent many hours on his back contemplating the missteps he'd taken to arrive where he was.

However, had they really been missteps? They were the path of the Goddess, just not the path that he'd intended. He had to keep reminding himself of that.

The problem was that he didn't know where he was going to. It was all well and good to be working with Judit and the others. However, they were all between things. This wasn't where he was meant to end up, was it?

Menefry had grown up on Calacktik, the home world of the Khanvassa. He'd never prayed to the representation of the Goddess on a Journey. He'd never wanted to leave his home. He'd always thought he'd find work doing security for a local business or perhaps even a temple, if he was lucky enough.

Yet, here he was, so many light-years away from all that he'd ever known.

Was his path to make it back home someday? In his heart of hearts, that was where he always saw himself going.

And yet…the Goddess appeared to have other plans for him. Someplace else for him to go, to protect this crew that were becoming friends. Good friends. Friends that you'd trust to wash your gossamer wings, the delicate set hidden beneath his hard shell.

So Menefry prayed for a more obvious path to open before him, willing for the Goddess to direct his steps, as always.

And in the meanwhile, he meditated on the nature of change and tried to be at peace with it.

CHAPTER 4

KIM

Kim had to admit that she was kind of, *sort of*, impressed with the Bantel section on the *Balmor* space station.

It appeared to have *everything* in terms of food, including her favorite donuts! She'd even shared some with Judit, who appeared to instantly become as hooked on them as she was.

While Judit and Saxon got them their next cargo run, Kim got to go play.

Alright, so she wouldn't actually tell anyone on *Eleanor* that she was playing. No, really, this was hard work! She needed to stay on top of her game, and she promised herself that she'd spend time schmoozing and networking after the main contest.

Which she admittedly couldn't enter, no matter how much she wanted to. They were still traveling incognito. Plus, if she won anything, that would draw too much attention to her.

Instead, she stayed with the audience in the theatre and oohed and ahhed with everyone else as the contestants were being put through their paces, showing off just how well they could blend into, well, everything. The stage was a few feet above where she was seated, in that perfect spot, a little ahead of the middle of the long rows of chairs, and a little to the side. The theatre was nicely warm, and had the smell of many Bantel in the same squished-in area—something slightly spicy and sweet.

Kim was honestly surprised at how good some of the contestants were. She had always considered herself one of the best.

Appeared that she was going to have to get some new gear, as well as up her game.

The final round were specialized environments for the three finalists. She scoffed at the female Bantel who blended into a forest background. Not only could Kim do that, she'd been regularly practicing on harder material.

The next contestant blended into an underwater scene, with lights occasionally flashing across the background.

While the guy did a good job, it wasn't very impressive, at least not to Kim. When would you ever need such a skill? If you were hiding underwater, well, you had to work with that. Not the background.

The third contestant, though, amazed her. It started off as a simple exercise, blending into a brick wall. She could do that. Hell, pretty much any teen could pull that off.

Then, the shadow of a plant was suddenly cast on the wall. The contestant recovered almost instantly, which was impressive. Still, something that most people could do.

However, a slight breeze started, so the shadow of the huge fern kept sliding and shifting.

And the contestant remained camouflaged.

That was truly impressive. It meant constant micro adjustments to mimic the moving shadow, while at the same time, maintaining the appearance of the brick wall.

He must have some special fabric that was helping him to do that. It was all Kim could think of. He couldn't be doing all of that on his own, could he?

And if he was, well, he'd just shown her some stunts that she hadn't even considered before. She always practiced against a static backdrop. She didn't stay still herself. It had taken quite a bit of work to be able to slide across something like sand or snow and not be seen.

What she was seeing today, though, was a whole additional level.

She was really going to have to practice a lot more to reach that. She couldn't wait to start!

After the contest had ended (the brick wall guy taking the main prize, of course) Kim flowed with the rest of the audience out into the exhibition hall, where numerous vendors sold pretty much everything one needed for improving one's blending skills. There were kiosks with video training with a whole series of more and more challenging backgrounds. More than one booth sold potions and pills to improve your speed at changing.

Kim had tried those, just once. While it had made her able to change so much more quickly, once the drug wore off she was sluggish for three days.

That would never do, particularly if she was on the run.

She paused at the suits which generated a cooling element, so that you could blend into the background and not set off any heat detectors.

She was pretty sure those were illegal, or at least frowned upon by most authorities—because really, what was the purpose of avoiding heat sensors and motion detectors unless you were someplace you weren't supposed to be? Then she realized that they had purposefully been weakened. They only worked for fifteen minutes.

It wouldn't take much to expand the life expectancy, just

add an additional battery pack. Which would mean more heat…

Clever way to get around the authorities and blatantly display products that most people had no need for.

Except, perhaps, people like her.

The exhibition hall wasn't that large, maybe only forty meters on a side. The ceiling was very high, probably so that the room could fit a show for one of the taller species. Tables and booths lined the walls as well as filled the center. Happy chirps filled the entire area. Kim practically skipped along as she shopped, going from one vendor to the next, collecting cards and contact information.

It wasn't so that she could go break into their factories later and steal some products. No, really!

Besides, they probably had really good security against someone like her. They knew who their customers were and who would be interested in stealing from them.

There was one guy she saw just sitting behind his table. No fancy displays. No loud music or dancing lights. Just a table, with a pile of cloth in front of him.

"So, what do you have on display today?" Kim came up and asked him.

All right, so she may have been a little too chipper. Maybe too many donuts for breakfast, along with the most wonderful sweet tea. Caffeine, sugar, and fat. The holy trinity.

The male Bantel looked her up and down. She preened. She was totally styling today in her green and red outfit. Her skin was a creamy yellow, while her eyes were pink. She looked good enough to eat.

Whereas this guy was wearing drab, dull cloth. It was all the color of one of Saxon's more boring vests. It was short sleeved, kind of baggy, with shorts. His skin was an interesting green color, more of a forest green than a spring green. But his eyes were plain black.

He just shook his head at her. "Don't think you'd be interested."

Kim stood there, a little stunned. "What do you mean? Aren't you going to try to sell me something?"

"Nope," he said.

That surprised her. Normally, the Bantel were known to be cheerful. Disgustingly so, at least according to Judit.

But this guy was being a real downer.

"Are you sure?" Kim said. "I might surprise you."

He gave her what looked like a sad, half smile. "All right," he said, sounding reluctant.

He pressed a button on a little disk that he had in his hand.

The drab fabric of his clothes faded away, along with *him.* Only his head, bare arms, and bare legs were visible. The rest of him had completely blended into the background.

"Ooohhh," Kim said, "that's awesome! Are your clothes made from this cloth?" she asked, indicating the pile of fabric on the table in front of her.

"They are," he said, tilting his head to one side. "I wouldn't think that someone like you would be interested."

Kim couldn't help but give him a huge smile. "You can never judge a person based on color." It was an old Bantel saying. Since they were masters at changing their skin color, one could never tell exactly the sort of person they were dealing with.

"True enough," the guy said. "I'm Dale. I'm the inventor of this new material."

"Wow!" Kim said. She came to stand beside him. "Tell me all the nerdy details," she insisted.

Dale gave her a shy smile, but complied.

Kim was already determined to buy as much of his fabric as she could afford.

Then maybe go and play some more…only this time with a companion. Dale was awfully cute.

CHAPTER 5

BASIL

Basil routinely hacked into security back channels at every station they went to. Most of the time, it was easy—much easier than it should have been. Particularly if the station was dominated by the Cartel. It was as if they were begging to be broken into, or arrogant enough to believe that no one would.

The *Balmor* station had been different. Instead of sliding right in, Basil found zieself on a side channel, almost as if the security system had expected hacking at the usual sections and had a redirect lying in wait for anyone who tried.

Basil was almost impressed. Almost. It only took a few more minutes on the computer for zim to bypass the side channel and hook into the main branch.

The chatter that flowed was mundane, as it usually was. People reporting possible crimes, security being called out to this section or that.

Basil stood in the new lab that zie, with the help of Menefry, had created. The primary engine room was a huge, echoing chamber that ran almost the entire width of the ship.

The two engine cores were on either side of the room, Which left a large, echoing space between them with not much in it.

Out of spare parts and some 3-D generated panels, Basil had built three sturdy walls that supported one another, then brought all zir equipment down here for running chemical experiments, primarily so that zie wasn't "stinking up" the rest of the ship.

The Oligochuno found very few chemical scents "bad." It was only when a scent would actually damage zir sensing array that Basil would characterize it as obnoxious.

However, both Judit and Kim had found the smells that zir experiments produced nauseating, so zie'd had to move zir lab down here.

The space had a hum to it, generated by the engines. Zie found it soothing, and so had moved more of zir equipment down here, setting up another work station for zieself. It was a little cooler down here than in the rest of the ship. That didn't bother Basil—zie just set zir own internal temperature up a bit. Zie found the polished floor a touch slippery, but again, zie just adjusted zir own segments to grip better.

Zie listened to the station security chatter in the background while zie continued working on zir current project: replicating the viscous glowing material that filled the tubes of the secondary engine system.

The experiments were going well. Basil had managed to isolate several of the key proteins that made up the substance. Of course, the fluid was organic in nature. But it had properties that Basil had never before encountered.

Basil was close to figuring it all out. Zie could tell that. However, how close was close? Was zie days away from finding a solution? Or years?

That was frequently the pace of all discovery: quick solutions at the start as the gross problems were resolved, followed by minute adjustments until the finicky solution was found.

Eleanor couldn't really help. Nor could Abban or Gawain. Eleanor was in charge of the primary engines and the ship itself. Abban used the secondary engines to somehow move the ship from ordinary space to hyperspace, while Gawain then used the secondary engines in a more normal capacity to propel them through hyperspace.

In the past, all ships had two engines, one for hyperspace and one for regular space. However, improvements to the design had allowed for those functions to be condensed to a single engine centuries ago.

At some point, could the functionality of the secondary engine be improved, so that only two individuals were necessary? One for the primary engines, and one for the secondary engines?

Zie understood, though, that would mean a change to the basic physiology of the Chonchu, the alien beings encased in an amber-colored substance in the heart of the secondary engineering room. They were a hive mind, and needed between three to five individuals working in concert in order to maintain consciousness and intelligence.

Could the current trio work as just a duo?

Zie couldn't even suggest that, however. Even hinting to Eleanor that perhaps she could be a duo instead of a trio first would bring confusion, then absolute panic.

Basil put aside the latest of zir experiments and looked up. Something had caught zir attention. At first, zie turned to look at the main engines. Even from where zie stood, zie could tell from the readouts down the sides of the huge tubes that everything was fine.

No one had come down to visit zim, no doors opening above zim, no friendly call from Kim or silent approach from Menefry.

No, it was the background chatter on the security channel. Zie was running it through a filtering program so that zie would catch anything potentially threatening to the crew or the ship. That hadn't caught zir attention though.

There was something in the rhythm of the security chatter itself.

Zie set up a quick analysis of the timing of the calls.

No one had such regular chatter. Every six, eight, or ten seconds, another burst of noise came through the channel.

There should be longer periods of quiet. Or quicker reports. It should ebb and flow like a wave, not be coming through like a regular pulse.

All the information zie was receiving on this channel was also fake.

Who would set up not one, but *two* fake channels for people like zim to hack into?

And why? What exactly did the station have to hide?

———

Basil recalibrated zir assumptions not just once, but twice as zie dug into the data.

It turned out that the *Balmor* space station had a *huge* Cartel presence. In retrospect, that made sense, as there were Chonchu here, as well as all the other races.

According to Eleanor, the Chonchu had at one point been more advanced than the other races in terms of working with hyperspace.

Then first contact had been made, with the Humans and the other races. The Chonchu had gladly agreed to be part of the Universal Trading Cartel so that they would have access to all those new markets.

However, the Great Plague swept over their worlds. Most of their queens died. A few, isolated, weaker queens survived.

The only way now for the Chonchu to access the rest of the galaxy was through a few carefully controlled hyperspace gates run by the Cartel. As well as to pay tremendous fees. According to the Cartel, that was to protect the rest of the universe as much as the Chonchu themselves.

Everyone had been made to fear the Chonchu, since they were a hive mind. Too many sensational reports had been released about the possibility of the Chonchu taking over the rest of the races.

It was all just static. Probably.

Basil was just the most recent of many who had speculated that the Great Plague hadn't been natural, but instead caused by the Cartel.

It appeared to be their MO. Anytime one of the races appeared to be getting ahead, something catastrophic would happen.

In recent history, first, it had been the Chonchu. Then the Bantel. Now, *Camelot* had been blown up, and the Yu'udir had taken it personally. Basil had read more than one backchannel report on the unrest on the Yu'udir worlds, how accusations against the Cartel had reached monumental levels. The various governments had shut down the protestors quickly, though. The Cartel could cut their worlds off too easily, leave them stranded, outside of all modern commerce and civilization.

That there were Chonchu on the *Balmor* station at all meant that it was very different than all the other stations.

And of course, that meant more Cartel personnel.

When Basil had finally broken through to what zie presumed to be the real security station chatter, zie wasn't surprised to find that it was encrypted. None of zir usual software made even a dent in the encryption.

It was as if the codes were based off something zie had no access to.

The only thing that wasn't encrypted at some level were names.

Zie had a list of them now. Most of them could be easily ignored, as they were the names of various Cartel members, or at least that was zir assumption. A quick search on most of the names had created an interesting matrix, one that zie didn't understand the ramifications of.

There was one name, though, that zie couldn't find any reference to. It didn't help that it was a single name, and had no other attached to it.

Sachiko.

Who was this person? And why were they so important?

Basil filled it away and kept zir algorithms banging away at the encryption. Maybe some year zie would figure out the code.

In the meantime, zie had more experiments to run.

CHAPTER 6
SAXON

"No," Saxon told Judit when she turned expectant eyes at him.

They were sitting outside one of the bars on the *Balmor* station that served a type of beer that both Humans and Yu'udir enjoyed. Though sections of the space station were open at all hours, there were parts that held to a Human twenty-four-hour clock, with the lights mimicking day and night. Judit had chosen this bar in part because of the beer, but in part because this section would experience something like night. All the lights had started to dim around 8 PM, and the ceiling had grown darker, with a pattern of stars splashed across it.

The bar itself was an interesting Human endeavor. Turquoise tiles done in a herringbone pattern covered the walls. Sections were cordoned off from each other by walls that were similar to lattice work, except they were done in a gold metal with open diamond shapes. The chairs echoed the ombre of light blue to dark, with some greens thrown in. Even the windows maintained the pattern, being triangular in shape. Only the ceiling presented a contrast, with large glowing ovals providing light.

Judit had chosen not to sit inside (for which Saxon was eternally grateful, given how uncomfortable those chairs looked) but to sit on the "patio" outside, the seating area just outside the bar blocked off from the passing pedestrians by a low fence, which, of course, was made out of metal with those same triangular shapes in it.

Saxon had been rather enjoying his porter, along with watching all the various people. It was nice to see such a mix of the races here. It had been fairly easy to get another cargo to take to a nearby system, as more than one of the races had delicacies that required the special containers that *Eleanor* had.

Then a group of three Chonchu walked by. He'd rarely seen a Chonchu up close before. Their bodies were white and fleshy, reminding him of a type of cod that he'd fished for as a boy. Though they'd supposedly descended from an aquatic species, they were still bipedal with two arms. Their noses were practically non-existent: like the Yu'udir, they didn't track their prey by scent. All of them had an elongated face, coming to a point above the forehead with a sharp chin below. They were hairless, and like the Bantel, their skin was covered in fine scales. They wore flimsy, gauzy material that floated behind them as they walked.

From the look on Judit's face, Saxon knew that she wanted to go and talk with them.

While she still felt guilty about having three people encased in amber in the secondary engineering room, Saxon had no such qualms.

Eleanor, Gawain, and Abban had made their choice to form the core of the spaceship *Eleanor*. They claimed to be happy with their decision. Saxon chose to believe them.

Judit still had doubts.

"No," Saxon said when she turned those pleading eyes toward him.

"I just want to talk with them," Judit whined.

Saxon shook his head and said, "No," again.

"But—"

"What would you say to them? You can't tell them anything about *Eleanor*. You can't ask them about Arthur's Project Nemesis. You can't see how they would feel if they were supposedly trapped on a ship. There isn't anything you can say to them," Saxon said. He tried to keep his voice gentle, but he could tell that his words still stung.

Judit sighed, her shoulders slumping. "I know what you're saying makes sense," she said. "I just, I just want to see what they're like. When they're not, you know, trapped."

"Weren't you the one advising that we needed to be cautious? That our luck was about to run out?" Saxon inquired dryly.

"I know," Judit said. She opened her mouth a couple of time, then shut it again, without saying anything.

Saxon took another sip of his excellent porter—dry with just a hint of chocolate at the end—and rolled his hand, a gesture to encourage her to continue.

"Look, I know this doesn't make any sense," she said. "I just have this feeling that we should talk with them."

Saxon gave her a very skeptical eyebrow. "I though the Bantel were the ones who got 'feelings' about things."

It was a low blow, he knew. Despite the fact that Judit knew that the Bantel weren't behind all of her woes, she still didn't trust them. She didn't care that much for Kim. However, she'd been making more of an effort to get along with their crewmate. She'd even gone so far as to spend a couple of hours in her off time hanging out with the Bantel in her own room, a "girls' night in."

Judit glared at him but at the same time merely said in a meek voice, "I know. I just can't shake the feeling, though."

That was unusual for Judit. She wasn't necessarily one to always go with her gut. But true hunters were born, not made. There was an instinct that went along with seeking prey that couldn't be taught, particularly when faced with a bleak winter, your clan starving, and no fresh tracks in the snow.

"All right," Saxon said. He grimaced, but took a much larger quaff of his wonderful porter, then put the mug down with a sigh. "Let's go talk with some Chonchu."

"Really?" Judit said, surprised.

"If you are feeling this strongly about it, then yes," he said, standing.

As they'd already paid for their drinks, Judit rose up eagerly with him. "Follow me," she instructed.

Of course. He should have known that she already had a course in mind. As they'd had to work more closely together on *Eleanor* than they'd had on the other ships, he'd come to appreciate that Judit *always* had a plan. Or four.

She was his pilot. And he'd hitch his ship to whatever star she chose to follow.

———

THE CHONCHU SECTION OF THE *BALMOR* SPACE STATION looked very much like the other sections. While *Balmor* was primarily a Human station, it had been built with the other races in mind, so even in the Human sections the ceilings and doorways were tall enough and wide enough for a Khanvassa.

However, it surprised Saxon to realize that the Chonchu were almost as tall as the Khanvassa, though they were skinny, like the Oligochuno. The loose fabric that they wore looked plain in the other parts of the station. Once they'd passed into the Chonchu areas, he realized that their garments actually had a sheen to them that made them sparkle in the appropriate lights. The colors were generally pastels: blues, pinks, purples, and greens.

They had no hair, which Saxon personally found off-putting. Their eyes were large and round, and tended to be black, though he'd seen individuals with other colors as well now, both dark brown and golden, almost a copper color. As far as he knew they had no sense of smell, and no real nose either. They tended to walk around with their mouths open, showing sharp pointed teeth which were only delicate compared to the Yu'udir's.

Judit marched them through hallways where clusters of Chonchu walked. He'd seen groups as small as three and as large as fifteen. Except for the dim lights, the hallways appeared to be the same as the rest of the space station. He kept expecting a fishy smell to be exuded from somewhere, but mostly the air smelled stale, as if it wasn't refreshed as often in this area.

Finally, they turned a corner and walked into what looked like an open market place. Shops lined the outside, while small kiosks filled the center. The walkways between them were crooked, with no straight path.

Judit turned and grinned up at Saxon. "This is the place," she said.

"I'm glad one of us knows where we're going," Saxon said dryly.

"Ah, come on. Just because we aren't going to the wrong side of the station for a fight or anything," Judit said.

"We need to keep our noses clean here, remember?" Saxon said. Really, when had he graduated to being the responsible one in their relationship? He was going to have to address that at some future date, do something wild and out of character. Or at least mostly out of character.

"I know," Judit said with a sigh. "This way."

Saxon followed Judit down through one of the twisting paths. Many of the kiosks were closed for the evening, with simple shutters drawn down over their merchandise. He didn't see any locks, which he found surprising.

Were the Chonchu so trusting that they didn't have to lock everything up over night? Or were there protections there that Saxon couldn't see?

They reached one of the open kiosks toward the end of the aisle. It was bigger than the standard size, maybe three of them put together, so at least eight meters long. Stools stood on one side of the white counter that ran the entire front of the shop, while a group of three Chonchu stood on the other side. A few of the stools were taken with a group of other Chonchu eating what appeared to be noodles.

The back wall, behind the counter, was a cheery red color, with white accents, and an open window in the center of it. He recognized the juice machines standing there, along with the usual urn for coffee. It smelled of lemon and garlic, setting his stomach to grumbling about the lack of recent food.

Judit slid onto a stool close to one end of the counter. Saxon took the seat beside her. At least it was tall enough for him and would probably support his weight. The Chonchu didn't have the muscle mass that the Yu'udir did, despite their height.

"We'll take two of the house special noodles," Judit said to the three Chonchu who had wandered over to take their order.

The three of them nodded together slowly, as if they'd had to wait while something translated what Judit had said.

However, once they had the order, none of them moved to start cooking.

It took Judit a while to realize what they were waiting for. "Here," she said, handing them a credit stick.

They again nodded as one, walked over to a debit machine, charged her something, then handed the stick back.

But still none of them started cooking. What was it that Judit had ordered?

Instead, the three of them stood staring at Judit and Saxon.

"Do you get many Humans through here?" Judit asked. She was trying to sound innocent, Saxon knew. He wondered if she had fooled the trio.

"Yessss," the one in the center said.

Saxon wasn't certain how to gender the Chonchu. Were all trios made up of the same gender mix as Eleanor, Gawain, and Abban? One female, one male, one other?

If so, then he decided that the center one, the one speaking with them, was the female, particularly given the pitch of her voice. She wore a gauzy gold-colored tunic. It didn't appear to be sewn so much as draped over her, then held with tiny bronze metallic clips at the waist. She had that same wide open gaping look of the others, her teeth like tiny needles. Her eyes were fathomlessly black, with no discernible pupils.

The one to her left was taller than she was, and broader, so possibly the male. The gauze he wore was more green than gold, and his eyes were more brown than black. His teeth looked the same as the others, though his mouth was notice-ably bigger.

The other was less defined. Zir face was more squished in, zir shoulders less developed. Zie wore purple-colored gauze that was less pinned, so it flowed when zie moved or used zir arms. Zir hands were longer and larger, with webbing between zir fingers and talons at the end of each of zir three fingers and thumb. Maybe that was the Abban of their group.

"We get a few Humans," the male said after a few moments. His voice was deep and resonant, and he spoke flawless Common. "We are in more than one of the Human books that detail the 'not to be missed' features of this station." He sounded proud about that.

"That was how I found you!" Judit gushed. "Said the house special noodles were absolutely amazing."

Still, no one had moved to actually make them any food. Or to call in their order.

Unless…were there people behind the wall, making the food? If they were all linked, one being as it were, as soon as the three out front heard the order, however many were in the back would have started cooking the dishes.

"How did you end up here?" Saxon asked, curious. He knew how difficult it was for the Chonchu to leave their world, bottled up as they were by the Cartel.

The female nodded at him. "Many Chonchu work here, on *Balmor* station," she said. She had a slight burr to her voice, making it sound raspy. While the male spoke effortless Common, the female seemed to have to pause more to find the words. "They want food from home."

Basil had talked with all of them about the number of spies that appeared to be on *Balmor*, the duplicated security systems, and how difficult it had been to hack into.

Were the Chonchu being trained as spies? Was the Cartel going to let them out of their cage? Or were they training others, other species, on the best ways to infiltrate the Chonchu homeworlds?

"What's your favorite dish?" Judit asked.

It surprised both of them when the third person spoke. Zie had a higher pitched voice, but Saxon wouldn't have sworn that it was female. "*Ulligulsum*," zie said. Zie appeared to laugh after that, exclaiming with a high-pitched, "Ha! Ha! Ha!"

"What's that?" Judit asked.

Saxon was already dreading the reply.

It was interesting—the Chonchu had almost no facial expression that he could read. Their mouths stayed open, their eyes wide. However, he noticed that their arms moved slightly as they spoke. Instead of being focused on the face, he turned his attention to their body language.

The female in the center just fluttered her fingers a little, while the male moved his wrists.

"Eel soup," the female finally replied. "Served cold. In aspic."

Cold gelatinous fish soup? Didn't sound tasty at all.

Then again, the Chonchu had come from an aquatic species, and their home world was mostly composed of oceans. Their preferred food was still fish.

"I think I'll pass on that," Judit said gamely. "Do you miss home?" she asked, sounding a bit more gentle. "Being away from everything you've ever known?"

Ah. That was why she came here. So that she could ask them about their loneliness, cut off from the queens.

The male answered. "There are some who miss home more than others." He shrugged, as the Chonchu had shoulders and that appeared to be a universal piece of body language.

The middle one spoke up again. "We have each other. We make home here."

"Good," Judit said firmly. "It's important to make your home where you are, find your own family there."

There was no reaction from the trio, but Saxon could feel Judit relax.

If the other Chonchu appeared to be happy on their

own, then that meant there was a good chance that Eleanor, Gawain, and Abban were happy as well.

The three shuffled off to the window, though Saxon hadn't heard anything. Two bowls were suddenly placed there.

So they must not be talking to a strict trio, but to a larger group, with more individuals in the back. Interesting.

The male picked up both dishes and brought them over to Judit and Saxon. The noodles looked plain, lightly covered in a red sauce. It smelled of fish and garlic.

The taste was spicier than Saxon had been anticipating. Fire at the start that mellowed out quickly. Of course, the meat was overcooked, but that was just him being picky. Not all races appreciated tearing into the raw flesh of their food, nor had the teeth for it.

"Very nice," Saxon said after taking a few bites.

Judit nodded her appreciation as well. "It's good," she said. "A little spicy."

For the first time, one of the group broke off from the others, the Abban of their group. Zie went over to one of the juice machines and poured pure water into two glasses, then brought the glasses back and put them in front of Saxon and Judit.

"Thank you," Judit said with a grin. "Do you often go off by yourself?" she said, directing her question at zim.

"Too often," the female confirmed. She stroked her long fingers down zir arm. "It worries me."

"Why is that?" Judit said.

Saxon nodded. He, too, was curious about that.

"Ha! Ha!" zie replied. "Irrational, they worry."

Was the worry irrational? Or did they worry about becoming irrational?

"Not important," the male said after a bit. "We are fine," he added, glancing over at the female.

Saxon wasn't certain, but that sure appeared to be a "we'll talk about this later" look.

It was something they'd have to ask Eleanor and the others about as well.

Saxon and Judit finished their meal, gushing again about how good the special noodles were, then started walking back toward the ship.

"Did you learn what you wanted to learn?" Saxon asked as Judit appeared to be deep in thought.

"Yes," Judit said. She grimaced at him. "And then some. There isn't much information about the Chonchu out there. Not many scientific papers have been declassified. There's much speculation about how the hive mind of the Chonchu works. And what happens to them when they're away from their clan for too long. If individuals left on their own lose their sanity."

Saxon nodded and kept pace beside Judit. He only felt a sliver of the worry that Judit did, but he understood her concern now.

No one knew much about the three aliens who formed the core of *Eleanor*. The people who might have been able to answer their questions had all been killed.

Was there a chance that Eleanor, Gawain, and Abban would go crazy after being apart from their people for too long? No longer communicating with the queens?

Saxon didn't have an answer to that.

No one alive did.

CHAPTER 7

CLAYTON

Clayton didn't consider himself a racist, or even a speciest. He accepted everyone on their own merits. It just happened that the majority of the important people in his life, those he trusted most, were Humans.

There wasn't anything deep or significant about it. It had just worked out that way. He felt perfectly comfortable with the other races. Growing up, he'd even had a friend who was a Bantel.

However, working so closely with one of the Yu'udir had certainly been an eye-opening experience for him.

For all that Fredrick sounded like a stuffy British professor, Clayton had expected him to be a killer at heart.

Except—Fredrick wasn't. He never moved in and made the kill.

No, Fredrick was a hunter. He'd turned out to be excellent at sniffing out the prey that Clayton sicced him on. But he never took that last step. He hung back at the crucial moment when he should have moved in. Even the times when he'd had Clayton's explicit approval, he'd still waited.

Clayton understood that the Yu'udir had "domesticated"

themselves as they'd advanced, becoming less warlike, more cooperative. Had all that killer instinct been bred out of them?

He was glad that he'd found Fredrick's weak spot, as it were. It made him easier to work with, and honestly, if necessary, it would make him easier to control as well.

Take that afternoon, for example. Clayton was in his office, with the windows showing a hologram of a sunset over the west Texas hills, long before they were civilized. Longhorn cattle mooed in the distance. He could practically taste the dust in the air, smell the dry brush and sage.

His heart occasionally longed for those simpler times, when a man fought against elements he understood, like a storm or the wind. Not faceless entities in a massive corporate structure who were trying to make a fool out of him, to strip him of his rightful power and place.

Instead of a horse riding across the prairie, he had a trusty hound tracking cyber scents.

Fredrick had come in for his usual mid-afternoon report. He carried with him a paper folder, as had become his habit.

The papers contained in there were generally of a highly sensitive nature, and Clayton would destroy them immediately after reading them. However, it was nice to have that touch, to have a physical connection with those faceless entities.

Oh, he could bring up their portfolios and look at the professionally staged photos that had been taken of his enemies. Or even look up a scandal page and seen what rumors had been posted about them, their marriages a sham or their children addicts.

Clayton didn't enjoy that much close contact. No, he'd rather be a sniper, shooting at people from miles away, surgical strikes, rather than an up-close and personal assassin.

Fredrick sat on the far side of Clayton's immense desk.

Clayton had brought in a special chair for Fredrick, one that better fit his massive size. While Clayton was merely average height for a Human, one hundred seventy two centimeters tall, Fredrick was at least two meters, possibly taller.

Clayton always tried to meet the Yu'udir while already seated behind his desk, just so he didn't have to strain his neck looking up.

Today, Fredrick wore a rather nice golden-brown tweed vest. When he was working at his desk, he had a matching flat cap that he also wore. Both were sophisticated products, meant to keep the Yu'udir cool.

Fredrick wouldn't have lasted a day out on the plains that Clayton loved, not unless he wore a special suit to maintain his body temperature.

Whereas Clayton was certain he could have toughed it out if he'd had to walk across one of the ice floes that the worlds of the Yu'udir were famous for.

Today, Fredrick had brought evidence of one of the competitors of Universal making some rather crafty deals.

Not that Universal actually admitted to having any competitors. No, they controlled the hyperspace gates, which meant they controlled all trade between systems. In some of the systems, Universal controlled all the local trade as well. Not necessarily by name, of course. Had to give people the illusion that they had a choice. Frequently, Universal did short and long runs in a system under different company names, which were in fact owned by Universal.

One of the little companies not currently owned by Universal, New Express Logistics or NEL, had decided that they wanted to branch out, and had started doing a lot of runs through more than one system. They were becoming known as the people to go to if you wanted to move cargo quickly and efficiently.

But at a price. NEL charged handsomely for such delivery.

Were they sustainable, though? That was the key. Universal built such a name for itself by its long term planning, twenty years out, not just the next quarter.

This little operation was eating into the profits of one of the local arms of Universal, despite being more expensive for shippers. NEL practically guaranteed a fast turnaround on any shipment.

On the one hand, it was good to see how a competitor innovated. Universal always stole from the best.

On the other hand, NEL was getting above themselves, and needed to be taken down a notch.

"Do we break them? Or buy them?" Clayton asked Fredrick after he finished his report.

Fredrick blinked, seemingly surprised.

He was such a good hound. But he never took that last, necessary, killer step.

"NEL won't sell," Fredrick said slowly after a few moments. "They pride themselves on their independence. They would take back ways and avoid using hypergates all together if they could, if there was another option open to them."

"Then it's a good thing there aren't any other options, isn't it?" Clayton snapped. "So we break them. Hire their chief logistics officer into one of the local companies owned by Universal. Learn as much as we can from him. Then start offering similar deliveries, only charge half as much."

Fredrick frowned. "The margins are already razor thin in most of those regions," he said. "Any local company would go broke quickly. It can't take up enough traffic to justify that sort of price."

Clayton smiled at Fredrick. It was a little sad, really, that the Yu'udir didn't see the bigger picture. "We can support them for long enough for them to kill the competition. Loan them money. Then they can raise their rates and pay us back."

Fredrick nodded slowly. "That's easy enough to do," he said. "But what is the long-term plan?"

"We are Universal," Clayton said. "That name, that brand, was chosen with deliberation and care. We will be a part of every transaction that is ever conducted across all of known space at some point." That had always been his family's goal. It wouldn't be achieved in Clayton's lifetime. But perhaps his heirs would get there. Or the generation after that.

The Universal Trading Cartel, to use the metaphor of the Khanvassa, was the Goddess of the Universe, and she would have one of her infinite fingers in every single pie.

"I see," Fredrick said. He sounded awed, possibly even reverent. "Thank you for sharing that."

He nodded and stood up, seemingly energized, ready to go and do the work of Universal. "I'll see that it's done."

He turned on his heel and walked out the door, his folder still in his hands.

Clayton smiled and sat back in his chair, enjoying the sunset shining through the holographic windows for a few moments, sipping his lemon seltzer water.

Universal. It was time the rest of known space understood exactly what that name meant.

CHAPTER 8

JUDIT

Judit met with the rest of the crew in the woods conference room. They were all gathered around the oval table, with a hologram of an amber-colored spire in the center, representing Eleanor, Gawain, and Abban.

Basil had finally gotten around to hacking into the hologram projected on the walls of the room so that it was at least a little less creepy. But only a smidgen.

She'd proposed going back to plain walls, but the rest of the crew had overridden her. Even Eleanor had preferred the woodsy background, despite the fact that she'd never seen trees like that before. Evidently, the sounds of quiet evening crickets were nice, as was the faint scent of pines.

Still, the trees that surrounded them were too closely spaced together, with impenetrable dark patches between the massive trunks. Though Basil had removed the red eyes that sometimes peeked out at them from the shadows, Judit couldn't help her instinctual reaction to keep checking over her shoulder, to make sure no one was there.

Menefry continued to use the desert conference room as his office. Which left the snowy one for Saxon. He used it as a retreat sometimes, getting Eleanor to crank down the temperature to what he considered comfortable.

So the woods conference room had become the usual place for gathering as a crew when there were decisions to be made.

Judit had an offer in hand from a little cargo company, New Express Lines, or NEL. They were offering a good—no, scratch that—a *great* bonus for quick turn arounds on cargo runs. However, they wanted to sign *Eleanor* on for a series of runs, not just a one-time deal.

It would really help their finances if they could take this contract. So much so, that Judit might consider a third 3D printer for the ship, for Basil to manufacture more parts for *Eleanor*. Maybe another EVA suit so that Saxon could help Basil.

Menefry had struck out so far on getting them some sort of cloaking device for hiding *Eleanor*, which would allow them to dig out of a system without worrying about someone seeing them. But a large part of their extra finances was allocated to his search.

They might have to go to a system that had recently bribed the Cartel with enough money to allow a war. Generally, the Cartel didn't approve of war. It messed with profits. However, every once in a while some poor ruler would get it into their head that they really, truly *needed* that other planet over there, and would bribe the Cartel to allow them to send troop transports through their hyperspace gate.

It always ended badly. The Cartel would lower the price of the bribes for the other system to send troops through, to counterattack.

Eventually, everyone would be decimated. Except that the pockets of the local Cartel personnel would be greatly enriched.

Since there was so little fighting anywhere, and the only

way to get from one system to the other was through the existing hyperspace gates, there had been very little need to develop cloaking technology.

That didn't mean that some people hadn't. It just meant that it was extremely difficult to come by. Menefry had another contact he was going to try.

In the meanwhile, they had this offer from NEL.

Judit had explained the contract. The bonuses for early completion were matched with a penalty if they were late. They wouldn't make any profit at all if they didn't deliver on time.

"Normally, I'd walk away from such a contract," Judit told the crew. "We've had a string of good luck. And *Eleanor* appears to be working, currently. But that just means we're due some bad luck. We could weather taking this contract and having *Eleanor* break down mid-way. Saxon and I arrange the cargo runs and I never ask the rest of you your opinion. Due to the amount of credits on the table, as well as having a stable series of runs, I figured I'd consult with you. Kim? What do you think? Is this a good idea? Or not?"

Kim looked startled, as if she hadn't expected to be called first. But Judit always called on different people to start.

The Bantel was wearing a dark brown shirt that almost, *almost*, looked normal. Except for the small neon green pinstripes that glittered and flashed whenever she moved. Her skin was actually a nice golden color for once, though her eyes made up for it, being a searing blue that somehow clashed with everything.

Before Kim spoke, she paused for a moment. Judit had come to recognize that as Kim doing a gut check.

No science had ever proven psychic ability (Chonchu and how they communicated notwithstanding). The Bantel were famous though for following their gut, and had better than average odds of being right.

It wasn't a huge advantage. But Judit would take whatever she could get.

"I say we go for it!" the Bantel enthused. "Particularly if it means coming back here. I met this guy," she confided.

"Oh?" Saxon inquired. If Judit was the head of the group and the pseudo-mom, Saxon would play the other parental equivalent.

"I showed you the cloth he invented, right?" Kim said, aiming for innocence but missing by a good meter or more.

Menefry suddenly leaned forward. He'd had his top set of hands folded on the table, but now stretched out with them.

"Wait," he said. "Dale invented that cloth?"

"He did!" Kim said proudly.

"Any chance you could get me the schematics for it?" Menefry asked. "We're still looking for a cloaking device. I've considered the need for commissioning one."

Judit cleared her throat. While it was good for the team to work together, they still had a decision to make that morning.

"Oh. Right." Kim sat up straight. "Even putting Dale to the side, I don't have any bad feelings about coming back to *Balmor* station."

"Thank you," Judit said. She knew she shouldn't feel as relieved as she did at the Bantel's announcement. She would never admit to anyone just how much Kim's assessment weighed in her final judgment. "Menefry?"

"I would like to come back here," the giant Khanvassa rumbled. "I don't see any reason why not to. I understand it means running with the same ship identity for a while. I think that's an acceptable risk for now."

"Basil?" Judit said.

The Oligochuno tilted zir head from side to side, the equivalent of a shrug for races that didn't have shoulders. "On the one sense, yes, I would like the contract, specifically for the things those credits could buy. On the other sense—as I said in my report, this space station has a *much* higher Cartel presence than I originally anticipated. I don't know for certain, but I suspect that they're running a spy school here. Possibly more than one."

Judit nodded. Basil had detailed out everything that zie had learned as well as some speculation about what the heavy security around the space station actually meant. Zie had done some casual examination of the interior of the space station, but hadn't found the hollow walls that generally made up Cartel space, such as they'd found on the *Gery* station.

Since the space station had specific areas for each of the alien races, zie had speculated that each section might have its own spy school, that were put into competition with each other on a regular basis.

None of them had had a chance to go exploring their specific areas enough to discover if this was the case.

"Saxon?" Judit said, turning to her co-pilot.

He nodded thoughtfully. "I've also read Basil's report. It's a lot of conjecture without much substance. Are we putting ourselves into danger by regularly returning to a Cartel-run station? Particularly one that tries to hide its Cartel presence? Yes, we are. Is it an acceptable risk?" He paused, thinking. "I believe so. I believe signing on with NEL for a few runs and getting enough credits to be comfortable is worth the risk at this time. This feels like taking the short run, as it were. The easy tunnel."

Judit nodded. She'd expected that would be his reply. "Eleanor?" Judit said, making sure that no one would forget that the ship was part of their *team*.

"I have no objection to returning here," Eleanor replied in her warm alto. "It would enable Basil to do some more repairs without having to use the EVA. I understand the risk, and I'm willing to take it. Plus, having a little bit of a more regular schedule, returning to a station we already know, would be lovely."

Judit sighed. She didn't feel the same way about that as the others, something she was well aware of. She preferred always going to new space stations, new systems. Short runs, not a long run.

But they were all here, stuck together on a single ship, a long run together, at least until they could clear their names. Which would only happen once the Cartel was no more.

"All right," Judit said after a few moments. "I'll sign *Eleanor* up as a NEL carrier, on a short-term contract. Menefry, you see if you can get us a working cloaking device. I would really like to be able to just disappear out of this system as needed, without drawing any undue attention. Questions?"

No one had anything else they wanted to chat about, so the meeting ended and the rest of the crew went on their way. Judit stayed in the conference room, still thinking.

"Anything the matter?" Eleanor inquired softly.

Judit had forgotten that the ship's representative was still there. "I'm afraid that we're going to run out of luck, soon," she admitted after a few moments. "Plus, there are some pretty hefty fines if we don't make a delivery on time."

"I see," Eleanor said. "As far as we can tell, the ship is operating fine. Not quite to full capacity, but much better than it was. Basil has done a good job at rebuilding our most fragile systems, making them more robust."

Judit nodded. She knew that. However, emergencies and accidents happened.

"Wouldn't it be better to run out of luck in a familiar place? Where it might be easier to obtain help?" Eleanor asked.

"True," Judit said. She hadn't considered that. It would

be easier to plan out scenarios if she already knew the layout and the players.

"We'll take this contract," Judit said slowly. "But you have to contact Basil or me the instant you feel something giving way or going wrong. I'll figure out a way to get out of our agreements." She might add a line or two about breaking the runs if the ship broke down.

Despite Eleanor's promises, and the rest of the crew's confidence, Judit still wasn't convinced that this contract was a good idea. But it was the best offer they'd had in quite a while.

Hopefully she was just being paranoid, and not precognizant.

CHAPTER 9

FREDRICK

FREDRICK SAT IN HIS TINY OFFICE AND LET THE hologram of data flow all around him. Streams of numbers and names tumbled out of the ceiling, from the walls, even rising up from the floor. They were color-coded for the various projects he'd been working on.

Sometimes he imagined that it felt like ants tickling his fur. Other times, it was a cool wind off the ice, stimulating yet soothing at the same time.

The hologram generator that he'd specially programmed to project the data was state-of-the-art. Clayton had okayed the expense without even looking at it.

Fredrick could only dream of having that amount of credits. He'd always been frugal with what he accumulated. He did have a very nice amount tucked away, but not enough.

Never enough.

What was enough? He'd always had a number in mind.

As with Arthur, *enough* would be the amount to buy his own space station. However, he wouldn't do anything as foolish as Arthur and set himself up as a target. No, he would never assume that he could be viewed as a *peer*. Universal, for all its PR about being the home for everyone, was speciest at heart.

Human to its core.

That was all right with Fredrick. He could work around that system until he could bend it to his will.

It was just going to take some time.

His office was tiny compared to the huge monstrosity that Clayton had. The walls were plain and covered with vid screens. Not so that he could show some stupid hologram of an over-heated plain that he'd die on if forced to live there.

No, so that he could watch and track more data.

The *data bath*, as he called it, was good for nudging coincidences together, those lines that had brought him to Clayton's attention in the first place.

He had a new line that he'd been pursuing, though he hadn't bothered to tell Clayton about it.

It appeared that one of those ships originally registered to the recently-departed Arthur had just signed a short contract with NEL, the freight line that he'd been concentrating on.

This meant that instead of chasing phantoms and ghosts, he had a good idea of where the ship was going, and more importantly, when it would return to a particular system.

Fredrick knew that Clayton believed Fredrick didn't have that "killer instinct" as the Human had called it.

Clayton was wrong.

The Human had no idea how often Fredrick had intentionally pulled himself back, how he'd looked to Clayton for confirmation and judgement instead of acting on his own instincts.

This time, Fredrick decided he would act. Particularly when seeing the streams of data, how the lines paralleled and marched together.

He was going to go to the *Balmor* station himself, see what he could of this ship.

There were ways of hiding the true registration of the ship. However, he had a visual record of most of the ships that had passed through the hypergates that had been in the Wolpol system, leading to and away from *Camelot*.

And while he could possibly trust someone with making this comparison, he would much rather do it himself.

Bring the kill to Clayton, instead of waiting to be told to "go fetch."

He shot off a message to Clayton that he'd gone off to do some research and would return in a few days. As Fredrick had already done this more than once, he wasn't worried in the slightest about it.

Perhaps this time, he would have news that would enrich his bank account with enough zeros to get by.

At least for a while.

CHAPTER 10

BASIL

Basil understood Judit's hesitancy about taking the contract from NEL. Having a predictable pattern or scheduled route for cargo made them, well, predictable.

Zie was more than willing to take that chance, particularly if it meant zie might finally be able to afford some of the equipment that zie desperately needed.

Basil hadn't forgotten about Kim, though, and her promise to not leave them high and dry unless they were comfortable and able to support themselves. Zie had had many late night talks with Eleanor, adding more precautions to her systems, making it even more difficult for someone to come in and steal her.

Eleanor would have to truly *want* to be stolen.

Zie hadn't really told the others the extent that zie had made the ship autonomous. There were only a few controls left to override the ship's ability to make its own decisions, fly where it wanted to, without any input from either helm.

Fortunately, Eleanor enjoyed flying with Judit and the others. Though Eleanor was capable of flight on her own, Judit had a natural flying ability that Eleanor was still learning. She explained it once as being born without a sense of touch, and that only now she was starting to learn where the edges of her body were.

That morning, Basil was working in the primary engineering room. The 3D printer was quietly clicking in the corner, printing out more backup fluid containers. Most of the original pipes in the secondary engineering room had been replaced. Only a few dark green patches remained, the rest a cloudy silver. Basil had improved the original design to be able to withstand the corrosive nature of the cooling liquid that the ship used, and so continued to swap out pipes.

While zie worked, as had become zir habit, zie opened up one of the encrypted security channels of the station and listened to it in the background. Mostly it was garbled nonsense interspersed with static and hisses, though the occasional word was clear.

It was bad enough hacking through the rotating ciphers that enabled zim access to the channel. That they'd also encrypted the chatter going through the channel was just pissing zim off. Zie was certain that the encryption rotated as well, which was why zie occasionally heard clear words.

Today, zie was fiddling with new code to try to break through the other security of the station. Zie had to be very, *very* careful not to leave any traces of zir passage through the network. Particularly since it appeared that the *Balmor* station had more than one spy network in place.

"What did you say?" came a quiet voice, interrupting zir concentration.

Basil shook zir head. Zir sensing ring didn't show anyone else in the space with zim.

"Yes?" zie said expectantly.

"What are you listening to?" Eleanor asked.

Basil drew a deep breath. Judit's talk of bad luck had made zim paranoid, even down here in zir lair.

"That's one of the security channels for the station," Basil said after a few moments.

"Huh," Eleanor said, sounding perplexed.

"Why?" Basil asked.

"Parts of it sound like our native language," Eleanor said slowly. She hissed out a few words.

"What did you just say?" Basil said.

"I just granted clearance to someone to enter a hallway," Eleanor said. "And this." She hissed again. "That's someone leaving a different section."

Basil tilted zir head to the side. "Is it all in your language?"

"No, just parts. Some of it sounds like scrambled up words," she said. She paused for a few moments. "And some of it is just nonsense."

"Are the scrambled words from your language?" Basil said.

"I believe so," Eleanor said. "It's like they took the fronts and ends of words and swapped them."

It made sense to use a language that most of the races had never heard of and had no access to. Anything computer-generated could theoretically be broken, eventually. Encrypting chatter with something that no one had access to would make it more difficult to break.

"I'm going to feed you the entire clip, all that I've recorded so far," Basil said. "Let me know what you hear, what you think is going on. This is only one of the security channels that I've been able to hack into. There are others."

"All right," Eleanor said.

Basil copied off the feed and sent it to Eleanor, then sat in silence for a few moments.

Zie should have thought of asking the Chonchu about

their language, as well as some of their codes. Eleanor wouldn't necessarily have been able to help much, that wasn't her area of expertise. Plus, while Eleanor was interfaced with a computer, she generally didn't use it for her "thinking."

With that in mind, Basil turned to the other channels, seeing if perhaps there were language filters that zie should be applying instead of merely algorithms.

It was going to take time to peel away the layers of security around the *Balmor* station. Fortunately, zie had a bit of time.

Zie was actually looking forward to returning here after their next run.

CHAPTER 11

MENEFRY

Menefry wasn't certain that he'd ever met a melancholy Bantel before. Most of them were chipper.

All right, so Judit was right and Kim could be downright annoyingly happy at times.

But Dale wasn't. His smile was sad, and he didn't talk in exclamation points. Menefry had done a small bit of hacking into Dale's background, and on the surface, he appeared to be exactly what he was, an unusual Bantel with a highly technical background in chemistry.

Given what they now knew of *Balmor* station, Menefry had passed the deep hacking to Basil, to see what zie could come up with. Menefry was good, but Basil was better. He might not have admitted to such a thing at the start of their journey together.

However, Menefry had learned that it was always best to allow the correct hand of the Goddess to move the pieces around, rather than trying to force it.

For now, Menefry was meeting Dale in his studio. Dale had agreed to take on the challenge of turning the camouflage material that he'd invented into a paint that could be applied to the exterior of a spaceship. Or possibly a net.

The cloth worked with a very low voltage of electricity applied to it. Micro-wires were woven in with the regular threads in order for it to work. Would they have to create a net of such wires and wrap those around the ship, then apply the chemicals? How would they hide the doors? The engines?

It was a technical nightmare, as far as Menefry was concerned. Still, Dale claimed to have made progress, so Menefry had agreed to meet him at his studio.

At least this time, Menefry knew better than to expect the walls and rooms of Bantel space to be as colorful as the inhabitants. The walls, floors, and ceilings were all an industrial gray with no features on them, all dials and readouts standing apart. By doing this, the Bantel wouldn't take it as a "challenge" to try to mimic what was there.

Dale's studio was in what Menefry would term a light industrial area. The neighborhood was close to the space port and full of warehouses. The walls and ceilings were further apart and wider than the domestic areas, so small shipping trucks could more easily trundle along with goods. Many of the buildings were featureless, no windows, just large cargo doors.

However, while the studio had the same sort of plain, beige walls, many windows had been cut into the sides. A small sign indicated that it was an artists' collective. He caught the scent of acidic paint as well as freshly cut wood as he stepped up to the door, examining the pad beside it for Dale's name.

Before Menefry could press the button, a small female Bantel came racing out of the door and collided with him.

"Oh, I'm sorry! I'm so sorry!" she proclaimed.

Menefry hadn't been expecting any attack. However, his body had fallen into instinctual patterns, and instead of being forced back, he'd merely spun with the weight that had slammed into him, all six of his hands forming into fists, his legs taking a wide stance, knees bent slightly.

"It's all right," Menefry assured her as he straightened up.

"I just wasn't expecting anyone there," the female said. She wasn't dressed as loudly as Kim normally did—instead, she wore almost all one color of dark green, while her skin was a lighter shade that nearly matched. Her eyes were large and brown in her face, and the ruff around the back of her neck stood up proudly.

Menefry patted down his sides, making sure that the Bantel hadn't "accidentally" lifted something like his i-stick. Everything appeared to be in place.

"You're sure you're all right?" she asked, peering closely at him.

"I am," Menefry nodded. He wasn't sure if her stare was because she was actually ascertaining if he was all right, or if it was because he was a Khanvassa. While all of the races certainly appeared to be well represented on the *Balmor* station, he'd seen distinctly fewer of his kind in this tucked away neighborhood.

"Good, 'cause I'm late for spy school," she said with a grin. "Bye!" she tossed over her shoulder as she ran off.

Menefry stood there for a moment, considering what he'd just heard.

Basil had speculated that *Balmor* had more than one "spy school" located in the various race quarters. This female hadn't actually meant that she was going to one, was she? Wouldn't it be a more hidden thing?

He pressed the button for Dale's studio, hearing the door click open just a few moments later.

Was Dale, too, part of a spy school? Except that being a spy meant not standing out, but blending in, at least as far as Menefry understood such things. And Dale stood out too much, being memorable because he was always sad. Still, Menefry was going to remind Basil about taking a deeper look at the Bantel, just so that they had a better idea of what they were dealing with.

———

THE GOOD NEWS WAS THAT THE MODEL THAT DALE HAD come up with had worked. The bad news was how expensive it would be for them to run wires that would withstand the cold of space across all of *Eleanor*.

However, it was a more effective system for a cloaking device than Menefry had ever heard of. The others relied on a projection system that was difficult to maintain in space. Whereas Dale's system would work even if sections of the ship were damaged. The Bantel had built in redundancy to his design.

If they used less wire, they could still get coverage, but if even a single wire was damaged, the cloaking device wouldn't work. By doubling the area of coverage, Dale ensure that the cloaking device wouldn't fail.

It really was just a matter of making the money to purchase the equipment at this point.

Dale's studio was an open area, with industrial pipes running across the ceiling, windows on one wall and racks of fabric on the other. The workbench in the center of the room was three meters on a side.

Dale had used a drone that was supposed to work outside of a spaceship and was therefore already able to handle the vacuum of space. It didn't match the exact silhouette of *Eleanor*, but Menefry assumed that wouldn't be a problem, as Dale had already taken into account repeater signals necessary to cover the vast real estate of the ship.

Menefry had followed Dale to a nearby airlock, used

primarily to launch such drones to do work on the station. He'd been the one to fly it away, then flipped the switch and watched it disappear. There was no possible way to track the ship once it had vanished. Heat sensors weren't any use. Mass didn't register.

It was a very effective demonstration of Dale's cloaking device.

Now, it was just a matter of cost. The amount of credits he'd asked for was easily three times what Menefry had access to.

And though Menefry was good at bargaining, he wished that Judit was with him, so that she could handle the final negotiations.

Menefry tried to bargain the Bantel down, but he wouldn't budge. The price he'd set was his first and last price.

With a sigh, Menefry turned away, ready to admit defeat, at least for the while. Though he would love to be able to say that they could afford such a cost, he knew that they couldn't. Not for quite some time.

"I would consider lowering my price by half," Dale said slowly before Menefry made it to the door.

"Really?" Menefry asked, turning back around.

Dale nodded. He looked more determined than he had earlier, even while stubbornly sticking to the price he'd quoted no matter how Menefry had tried to talk him down.

"Yes," Dale said. "If you'll take me with you."

"Excuse me?" Menefry said, not sure that he heard Dale correctly.

"I can't...I can't stay here," Dale said after a few moments. "I want to go someplace else. Start over."

"And?" Menefry asked, walking slowly back to the huge workbench.

"You could always use an extra pair of hands on the spaceship, right?" Dale said.

"Extra hands means splitting the profit we make into more pieces," Menefry replied.

"True," Dale said, nodding. "But with my device on board, you'll be able to slip in and out of systems unnoticed, which could bring a higher return, yes?"

Menefry tilted his head back and forth. "Maybe. Maybe not," he said. "But why?"

"The first price I quoted you will get me out of here in style," Dale said. "It means that I could start over, but not from the ground floor. It means getting myself to a new system and getting all set up. I don't have to scramble for new clients from day one. I can breathe a bit after such a move."

"All right," Menefry said. That made sense to him.

"The second price, well, that means I land poorer. Without as many resources. Not paying for the cost to ship everything would help. Plus, it means I actually do leave. I can't put it off, and put it off, until I'm suddenly left with no money and am still stuck here in this station."

"So the second price is motivational," Menefry said, wanting to make sure that he understood the gist of what Dale was asking for. "It isn't so much about the money, as expectations at that point."

"Exactly," Dale said, nodding emphatically. "I'd have to leave, because that would be part of the contract."

"Why do you want to leave so badly?" Menefry had to ask.

Dale gave him a sad smile. "You can't love a spy," he said simply.

"And?" Menefry prompted.

"I tried. But they build their lives on deceit. It's why Kim, as lovely as she is, could never be a partner to me either. She's a thief, no matter how she might try to deny it. I need someone who can live an honest life with me," Dale said.

Menefry wondered how many of the Bantel were actually involved in the spy trade on *Balmor* station, or if Dale had simply had a run of bad luck.

"How long would you stay with us?" Menefry asked. He had no idea if he'd ever be able to talk any of the crew into it. Particularly Judit, given her innate dislike of the Bantel in general.

"Eight trips," Dale said decisively.

As the Bantel only had four fingers on each hand, their mathematics system was base eight, unlike the Humans and Yu'udir, who used a base ten. The Khanvassa used a base eight system as well, despite only having six limbs, because of the Goddess. Whereas the Oligochuno used a system of base twelve.

He had no idea what the Chonchu used, but he would suspect it might be based on some sort of three, the minimum unit they needed.

"I cannot make this decision on my own," Menefry said with a decisive nod. "I will go and talk with the others. I don't know if they'll go for either solution," he warned.

"I think they might," Dale said. "I think the advantage of having the inventor on the ship with you while trying out such equipment on a series of runs would outweigh their objections."

"You might be right," Menefry said.

They said their goodbyes and Menefry started walking back, out of the industrial areas and to the port itself, where *Eleanor* was parked.

Would they agree? Was there any way to swear Dale into secrecy? How could they trust yet another person in this conspiracy?

Menefry didn't know.

The ship was in a huge hangar. The floor itself was magnetic, as there was no gravity in the hangar. The ships in here could never land anywhere with full gravity. Not that they couldn't withstand the effects of the gravity, but they didn't have the feet to support themselves—no landing gear.

Basil was scooting around *Eleanor*, and appeared to be unhooking the ship from the floor.

Were they taking off? That was unexpected.

Judit stood just to one side. "Good. You're here. We're leaving. Now."

"What happened?" Menefry asked confused.

Judit sighed. "It's Saxon. His brother was killed. We're breaking our contract and heading to his home."

Menefry sent off a quick note to Dale letting him know that their circumstances had dramatically changed, but that they'd be returning soon.

Just when, Menefry had no idea. But hopefully, they would come back.

CHAPTER 12

SAXON

Saxon appreciated that Judit left him alone for most of the trip to Yau'Mrapa, the planet where he'd been born and raised. All he felt was numbness. His brother had been so alive. Silly. Funny. The class clown. How could he be dead? It was unreal.

He sat in his rooms, in one of the big chairs, and stared blankly at the walls. Quiet music played in the background, a grandiose opera about lovers fatally trapped on a dying planet. He supposed it was slightly better than the lugubrious adolescent poetry that he tended to read. But not by much.

They'd made all the arrangements for when they arrived. Saxon and Judit would go down to the planet while Basil, Menefry, and Kim would stay with the ship.

What would Judit think of Orwed, the tiny town Saxon had left as soon as he could? She'd probably complain bitterly about the lack of a rough side of town or the bad side of the spaceport. Not that she'd be looking to get into a fight.

Although, it might be interesting to set her against a group of good ol' boys who thought they were all that, only to find their asses handed to them by a Human woman.

Might do them a world of good.

However, Saxon didn't anticipate being on the planet surface for much more than twenty-six hours.

He figured that Judit might appreciate Orwed, at least in terms of comparing it to where she'd grown up. It had been one of the things they'd bonded over, early in their friendship: the need to leave the small town of their home.

It would be mid-spring there. There would be a good chance of snow some nights. Not a large amount, just a footprint of snow. The air would be crisp and cool, the skies blue. Fields surrounding the town would be planted, and there would be flowers poking up. Migratory birds would be rushing back, and the sound of their calls and songs would be everywhere.

Mostly, Saxon tried not to think or worry too much. Tried not to imagine Maxwell's children, how much shock they must be in, to lose both their parents. His sister, Flora, was going to take the children in, of course. It would be a shock to her family as well, but better that than leaving them with strangers.

Both Maxwell and Flora had known that Saxon had survived the destruction of *Camelot*, despite accepting the insurance money that had been paid on his death. (The larger share going to Maxwell's family, as he had two children and Flora only the one.) They also understood his need to stay away, how important it was for them to maintain the fiction that he'd died. The children were their first priority, and anything that might possibly endanger them was not to be tolerated.

However, Flora had demanded that Saxon return home, at least for a short while, after the death of Maxwell. She assured him that they'd keep his return hidden from the children. But she'd insisted that he come home.

Saxon and Flora had never been close. She was ten years

his senior, eight years Maxwell's. It had always been the two boys versus her, those few times Saxon really remembered playing or being with her.

He'd been six years old when she'd gotten jobs and started working outside the home. He'd been eight when she'd moved out. They'd never really reconnected as adults, as Saxon's first real job had taken him off-planet and he'd never returned for an extended stay.

Maxwell had gotten to know their sister as an adult and had grown to like her. Though he did sometimes complain that she was a bit too traditional. Saxon would just take his brother's word about it, that she was someone worth knowing.

It had been a freak accident that Maxwell and his wife had been killed in, nothing suspicious had happened or that would cause any concern: a drunk driver plowing into their vehicle on a back country road.

All the modern safety features couldn't protect you against idiots who had deliberately disabled theirs. At least it had only been the parents who'd been killed, the children at home for the evening.

Now that the initial shock had worn off slightly around the edges, the pain of Saxon's grief spreading like thin ice through his system instead of a talon wedged somewhere in his heart, he'd started to wonder why it was that he was going back to Orwed. His sister, the matriarch of the family, had asked him to return. However, there really wasn't anything there for him.

And yet…he hadn't fought her demand. There was a part of him that really needed his family, those he'd been born with, around him. The crew of *Eleanor* was like a second family, but they were still coming together. Still learning each other's ways. Still figuring out how to support each other, particularly in a time of crisis.

For now—Saxon let the music in the background weep the tears filling his heart. He'd cry his own tears when they reached the planet and he saw Flora again.

And afterward…hopefully his new family would still be there for him as well.

CHAPTER 13

JUDIT

Judit had been born on a space station and had spent most of her forty-odd years in space. She could count the number of times she'd been on a planet just using the fingers of one hand.

She didn't *like* planets. They were big, messy, and too easy to get trapped on. Weather! There were no handy escape pods, no easy-to-sneak-aboard ships. The space port had been half a day's travel from the Podunk small town they'd ended up in. Ordwel. Or whatever *friss* hell this place was called.

They'd had to hire a driver to take them to Saxon's hometown. None of the automated services had a convenient schedule, only running every other day or so.

Seriously. And she'd thought she'd grown up on the ass end of nowhere.

The driver let them out on what was supposedly the main drag of the town. At least there were some buildings nearby. The last few hours all they'd passed had been empty fields full of something green and growing.

It wasn't that Judit was agoraphobic. She just wasn't used to so much open space stretching out around her forever. As well as all that sky above her. No comforting ceiling, no tunnels or hallways. Just space. Empty space.

"Breathe, Judit," Saxon said dryly from beside her.

"I am," she replied, but softly. She didn't want to argue with him. She was here to be supportive, she reminded herself.

"Now what?" she said, looking around. There were stores up and down the street. A bakery nearby that surely sold some sort of fried bread or donut. She wasn't sure if the bars were open or closed. They all looked dim and dark—her kind of place—but she figured none of them would carry anything she could drink.

Besides water.

A couple of small vehicles puttered by on the street. Enclosed vehicles that rode on four wheels instead of floating or flying. They appeared to come in a variety of different colors and lengths, though they were all about the same height. Some had two doors, others had four. Not a moving sidewalk in sight. People had to walk everywhere.

Weird.

"Flora said she'd meet us at *The Tower Bakery*. We're a bit early," Saxon admitted. "This way."

He walked a bit further up the sidewalk. Judit could smell so many different things on the cold air. A sweet perfumed scent—possibly from the colorful sprays of flowers hanging off the street lights. Another deeper, mustier scent that was probably the dirt from the nearby fields. An ozone-like scent that was probably the electric vehicles.

And then—yes!—that tantalizing smell of baked grains.

"After you," Saxon said, opening the door for her.

Judit passed inside but then stopped, drinking in the heavenly scents.

It looked sort of like a normal bakery, the kind she'd find on most any space station. Big glass case up front stuffed with baked goodies. Right behind that, on the counter, an altar to the only god the Yu'udir and Humans shared: a huge shiny coffee maker with a roast that didn't smell as if it had been burned to a crisp. A few large tables scattered across the floor, though when Judit adjusted the scale up from Human to Yu'udir, they were actually kind of small tables. No one else was in the shop, just a younger Yu'udir who came out from behind the back and awaited them at the counter.

The primary difference was that in addition to pastries, there was a whole second case with heated trays and barely cooked meat. While the Yu'udir could stomach some vegetable matter and grain, the primary element in their diet was dead critter. They had never been able to adapt or become more omnivorous, unlike the Humans or the Bantel.

There was no such thing as a vegetarian or vegan Yu'udir. Not unless they were crazy.

Saxon walked up to the counter and ordered them… something. She'd heard him speak his native tongue before, but it primarily had been the pair of them exchanging insults and curses. The teenaged Yu'udir from behind the counter got them two cups of coffee along with a cup of water for her to make hers palatable, two sausages, and a single puffed-up square pastry that oozed a red sauce out the corners.

Saxon paid using the generic i-stick that Basil had concocted for them, something untraceable, before collecting all the food and settling them at a table that looked out over the main street.

Before Judit could question the intelligence of sitting someplace where people could easily see them, Saxon said quietly, "No one will recognize me. Not like this." He indicated his rather natty golden vest and flat cap.

Judit looked back at the teenager behind the counter. He wore what could best be described as a flannel shirt, done in a red and black check, that looked fuzzy and warm. The hat he wore was more like a Human baseball cap, that he wore backwards on his head, the wide brim hanging over his neck.

Before Judit could reply, another pair of teenagers came in. They really only had eyes for each other, not the strangers sitting in the corner. They, too, wore flannel shirts and baseball caps, though the colors and size of the checks were different.

"So what should I offer as a bribe to Flora for pictures of you in flannel, instead of tweed?" Judit teased as she took a sniff of her coffee.

Whoa. That was strong enough to win a space battle on its own. She hastily added a bit of water to it before it decided to climb up out of its cup and strangle her nostrils.

"I was always dignified, no matter what colors I wore," Saxon told her stuffily. He ruined the effect by tearing into one of the sausage links, then giving a very soft moan. "I'd forgotten how good these were," he admitted.

Judit took a bite of hers. The meat was gamey, the Yu'udir equivalents of garlic and pepper overwhelming. But by the second bite, it had started to grow on her.

She put that to the side and reached for the sweet instead. Sugar covered the top of the puffed-up pastry square. She tore it in half (because really, all eating utensils were for sissified city folks, not for these good-hearted country bumpkins) and licked her fingers clean of the sweet berry jam that flowed out.

The pastry dough was flaky, and had a harder crunch than she was expecting as she bit into it.

Saxon grinned at her. "It's called a 'bird's heart' pastry," he said. "It's supposed to be reminiscent of crunching bird bones."

"I see," Judit said dryly, determined not to be put off. In many ways, it was typical of all things Yu'udir—despite their air of civility, they had determinedly held on to their more barbaric past, even more so than most Humans.

They ate a few more bites in quiet before the door to the bakery opened again.

Judit couldn't articulate how she knew that the tall female Yu'udir who'd just come walking in was related to Saxon. Maybe it was the searing blue eyes, though many Yu'udir shared those. Perhaps it was the way her black face crinkled along familiar lines. Or maybe it was just the way she held herself, a confidence and quiet strength that Saxon always exuded.

She came right over to their table. Both Saxon and Judit stood up at her approach. Saxon clasped arms with his sister, then leaned forward slightly to touch foreheads.

Judit knew that Saxon would and could hug, he had done it to her in the past, particularly if they'd both had a bit too much to drink.

The forehead touching was a bit more formal while at the same time, a bit more intimate.

Flora also wore flannel, though hers was bright yellow and black checked. She didn't wear a hat. She did have a rather large pale green bag slung over her back. Judit would call it a "mom-purse." It probably contained enough of an emergency kit that Judit could land on a hostile planet and survive.

Flora said something in Yu'udir, which Judit took to mean that it was good to see him, or something similar.

"I'd like you to meet the captain of my ship," Saxon said, switching over to Common. "This is Judit Kovács. Judit, this is my sister and eldest sibling, Flora."

"Pleased to meet you," Judit said, nodding to Flora. She wasn't sure how else to greet her. Handshakes were Human in nature. Clasping arms would feel as though she was assuming too much.

"Likewise," Flora said. "You always did have a fondness for *jagenoorlu*." Her accent was less scholarly than Saxon's, more brusque. She glanced at the table.

Saxon just grinned at her. "Want me to get you one?"

Flora rolled her eyes at him.

It made Judit's heart lighter to see the siblings teasing each other.

Flora went to get her own cup of coffee, then sat. Saxon started asking about the family, shared acquaintances. Flora had many stories that left Saxon chuckling.

Judit didn't try to intrude. This trip was for Saxon, for him to heal. Losing Arthur and the dream of *Camelot* had hit him harder than the rest of them. Losing his brother so soon afterward had just poured salt into the still-open wounds.

"But you'll be able to meet all of them soon enough, for dinner," Flora said after a few moments.

The stillness that formed around Saxon was colder than a sudden freeze.

"No, I can't," Saxon said after a few moments. "I am not about to endanger the family. It was bad enough that I came back to Orwed."

"You aren't here to rejoin the family?" Flora asked. There was an odd intonation to the words, as if this was a ritual request.

"I cannot," Saxon said emphatically. "Not at this time. It isn't safe. My enemies may try to use my family against me, if they know I'm still alive."

"What enemies?" Flora said. It wasn't quite a sneer, but it was dipping into that territory.

Saxon sighed. "I escaped the destruction of *Camelot*. I wasn't supposed to."

Judit could see that Flora wanted to argue with her brother, possibly bully him into coming back home regardless.

"We are working to clear our name," Judit said softly. "Hopefully, there will be a time in the future when we can return to living openly."

Flora pressed her lips together and merely glared at the pair of them. "Then why come back at all?" she finally said, turning her piercing gaze on her brother.

"Because you asked me to," Saxon reminded her quietly.

While Flora's accent had been getting harsher during the course of their conversation, Saxon had started sounding more and more stuffy, as though he exuded tweed from his very pores.

"I asked my brother to come *home*," Flora said. "I didn't ask him to visit."

"It isn't safe for me to stay here," Saxon said. "It isn't safe for you. Or the family."

Judit's i-stick vibrated *hard* in her pocket, three sharp, short bursts.

The only one who would send her a message here would be from the ship.

She pulled it out of her pocket and glanced at it while Saxon continued to argue with his sister.

"We have to go," Judit said, abruptly standing. She glanced at Saxon. "We were followed here."

Saxon looked perplexed but he rose from his seat. "Okay," he said slowly.

"Basil tracked a ship that came after us from *Balmor*," Judit explained.

"You're sure it wasn't coincidence?" Flora said, sounding as if she didn't believe them.

"Not without some sort of direct confrontation, no," Judit said. Before Flora could start arguing, Judit added, "But what business would a private Cartel courier ship have in this sector?"

Flora opened her mouth, then shut it again. "I see," she

said. She turned to Saxon and said firmly, "I will not ask you to return again. However, you can do as you see fit."

She rose from her chair without another glance at Judit, then turned and swept out of the bakery.

Saxon pulled himself up stiffly, frozen in place for a moment. Then he shook his head and pulled out his own i-stick, typing quickly. "The driver who brought us here hasn't left yet. He'll be outside in five minutes. Drink up." He quaffed his own coffee and hurriedly tore into the remaining sausages, while Judit ate the rest of the pastry.

In just a few minutes, they were outside, back on the street corner they'd been dropped off at.

"I must apologize for bringing us on such a fool's errand," Saxon said, his eyes on the far horizon. He was holding himself so stiffly his bones must hurt from the effort.

"Don't be," Judit said sharply. "The Cartel is on to us, which was something we had only suspected before. Now, we know, and it doesn't matter what registration we use for the ship."

"What are we going to do?" Saxon said after a few moments.

Judit took one last deep breath of what she could only call "colorful" air—filled with so many natural scents.

She'd trade it for a good set of scrubbers and actually *clean* air any day.

"Now, it's time for the pursued to lay a trap."

CHAPTER 14

KIM

The space station orbiting Saxon's home planet was called *Dedmund*. It even sounded like a stuffy professor who spent all of his time in a library studying instead of out having a good time.

Still, Kim was determined to enjoy it, as she was really the only one of the crew who'd been allowed to go onto the station. The rest were all floating in space on *Eleanor* since Saxon and Judit had returned.

Kim took it as a great honor that Judit would trust her with this, ignoring the fact that if she screwed up, she'd be the one left behind.

Except that Judit would come and rescue her. She was like that. Kim wasn't sure what it said about her that she'd never even *known* someone like that before. She'd been on her own for so many years, without a partner, let alone a team. But the last time Kim had screwed up, Judit and the others had come for her, broken her out of that awful place.

Not that she still had the occasional nightmares about being chained to a table with a mostly-invisible monster breathing right behind her. No, not at all.

However, this time, Kim wasn't about to screw up.

The courier that had followed them was registered to the Cartel, to one of the directors of the board, through a series of shell companies that Basil had torn through, eventually coming up with the name Clayton.

Of course, no one expected an actual member of the board to be here at this space station. However, watching whichever one of his minions who was there and getting some more information would be useful. Or at least a good first step.

According to Basil, the security on the *Dedmund* station was laughable. Particularly after the *Balmor* station.

Kim was happy that they'd be going back to *Balmor*. There *had* to be some excellent thieves there, plying their craft. She just had to sit in a public place and watch them work their lifts and placements.

In the meanwhile, she got to practice some of her own.

The single person in the courier ship was a Yu'udir, which had drawn doubt on whether or not he was actually following them or not.

However, Kim had a *feeling* about this, about him, about that ship with the innocent enough registry number of *CP-703*.

It hadn't taken much hacking on Basil's part to get Kim to show up as working for the Cartel as a security/customs agent. That Judit had already located where Kim could steal a uniform that would fit her on the station was impressive.

Except that Judit was like that as well, always knowing where the most logical place for supplies was likely to be.

The blue uniform was just *icky*. The cloth was harsh against her skin, and having to wear the same color every day? Ewww. Likely to make her suicidal. Or homicidal. Xenocidal? Something.

She sat in the workers' cafeteria, her paperwork claiming

that she'd just transferred into this tiny station despite having several years' experience.

Seemed that she must have slipped up enough at her last post that they'd transferred her rather than deal with the problem. Or at least that was how Judit explained it.

The cafeteria was actually kind of nice. It had a great view of the planet below, all blue and white and cold. The tables were a neutral beige and the chairs could be adapted to whatever species happened to be using them, with telescoping legs so she didn't feel like a little kid sitting at a table made for adults.

There were three other Bantel in the cafeteria, and she'd seen a few more on her way to "work" that morning. Of course, most of the people she'd passed were Yu'udir, with a smattering of Humans, followed by one or two of the other races.

But no the Chonchu.

Honestly, Kim found herself getting angry every time she thought about how the Cartel kept the Chonchu bottled up. It wasn't fair, it wasn't right, and when she had enough money and influence, she might actually have to go do something about it.

If Judit, or someone else on the crew, hadn't already beaten her to it.

Kim sat quietly nibbling on the fried pastry that she'd found on the cafeteria line. All the foods were color-coded for the various races, though it was pretty easy to tell which ones were mostly for the Yu'udir, as those tended to be huge vats of barely cooked meat. As well as coffee.

Ewww.

And there was her target. Seemed that this guy, Fredrick, was pretty frugal, private courier ship notwithstanding. Then again, he surely wasn't paying for that, but had expensed it.

He looked kind of like he belonged on a station called

Dedmund. The other Yu'udir either wore flannel shirts that looked pretty comfy, or they wore the sort of tweed vests that Saxon favored.

This guy would wear tweed upon tweed. The vest was a shade of Cartel blue, clearly showing where his allegiance lay. He didn't have on the ubiquitous flat cap, but she knew that he must have several matching ones. His fur was brighter than the Yu'udir around him. Probably had a special salon that he went to regularly to get it washed and fluffed up.

She would say that the talons on his hands were shorter and more blunted than the others. And he ate with less gusto than any of the Yu'udir surrounding him.

Somehow, that made her even less trustful. As if hiding his true nature, pretending to be more civilized, made him much more dangerous.

Her stomach rolled in a way that told her that this was a *bad idea*.

Should she just leave? Not try anything?

No, she would just have to go with plan B, and hope that Basil and the others would be okay with that.

Kim dallied over her own juice, which appeared to be fresh squeezed from a plant native to the planet below. It was both sweet and tart, with a lovely purple color. She was going to have to try changing her skin to that color someday.

When Fredrick rose to carry his tray back to the kitchen, Kim did as well. She placed herself deliberately in his path, though to the casual observer, it would all be an accident.

She didn't mean to bump into him so hard. No, really!

The distraction worked, though, and Kim walked away from the encounter with Fredrick's i-stick.

Hidden on the belt of her uniform lay a long, cloth-covered tube. Kim stuck the i-stick into it as she kept walking. She only had a few seconds or the target would be out of range.

A faint click told her that the reader that Basil had invented had done its work.

Kim turned and started following Fredrick. She bent down as if picking something up before she said loudly, "Excuse me, excuse me!" as she hurried up to Fredrick. "Did you drop this?" she asked innocently enough, holding out his i-stick.

Fredrick looked startled. He patted the pocket of his vest and found it empty.

Kim maintained her innocent, wide-eye stare at him.

"Yes, I must have," Fredrick said slowly. He didn't take the proffered i-stick, however. "Who are you? What is your name?"

"Riley," Kim chirped up at him. "I'm new here," she admitted. "Just started last week. What's your name?"

"Riley, hmm?" Fredrick said. He finally took back the i-stick and pointed it at the badge Kim wore.

All the information came back clean, that much Kim knew. She didn't know how deeply Fredrick would go delving, or how good the background was that Basil had developed.

"You're here from the *Balmor* station?" Fredrick asked, supposedly reading out the information that was displayed on the side of his i-stick.

"No, I'm here from the *Niocia* space station," Kim said. That was what Basil told her. Right?

"Oh, right, my mistake," Fredrick said. He gave a patently false smile to her. "Thanks for returning this."

Kim just shrugged. She stood there for another awkward moment before she waved at him. "Time for my shift!" she said cheerily.

Then she made herself turn and walk away, feeling his eyes boring into her neck like some kind of monster was behind her.

It wasn't until after she was at her desk that she finally sent a message to Basil and the others that they might have a problem.

CHAPTER 15

FREDRICK

Fredrick ran every sort of security check he could on his i-stick, searching for some sort of hidden tracker or extraneous software that might have been injected into it.

However, he couldn't find anything. No spurious programming had been added to his i-stick during the few moments it had been out of his control. As far as he could tell, no one had touched his accounts. He had, of course, already changed all his passwords, so whatever public information had been gathered from it was already useless.

The i-stick was clean.

Why had that Bantel stolen it? What had she done with it for the few seconds that she'd had it in her possession?

He'd gone back and checked the recording of the encounter.

Whoever she was, she was good. Only after he'd slowed down the video could he even see her hands move. Plus, she appeared to have just held it to her side for a few moments before turning, supposedly picking it up, then bringing it back to him.

There was something more going on here. What exactly, he wasn't certain.

At the first encounter, the one that had brought Fredrick to the attention of Clayton, there had been a Bantel involved.

Coincidence?

Possibly, but unlikely.

Particularly when combined with the fact that the ship he'd been tracking took off shortly after the encounter he'd just had.

Though he brought up pictures of the two and tried to compare them, facial recognition for Bantels was still an evolving science, as they could change not only their coloring, but the really good thieves could also change the size of their noses, the hollowness of their cheeks, the pointedness of their chins. Rumors abounded that some could even shrink or grow the size of their neck ruff, changing in appearance from male to female in a matter of moments.

The facial recognition gave him a sixty-seven percent chance that Riley and the Bantel who'd been in custody were the same. Not enough to be certain.

He started going through records, assuming that Riley, or whatever her name actually was, would also be long gone after their encounter, disappearing in a matter of minutes. Supposedly, she was some sort of customs agent, who dealt with licenses and goods going in and out of the system.

Strange. As far as he could tell, the Bantel was still here, on the *Dedmund* station, even hours later.

If she was part of that other crew, she should be long gone.

He left the small office he'd been using and actually walked over to where Riley was supposedly working to verify that she still existed.

The area was quiet, despite being a large open space

broken up with moveable walls and desks. It was only when Fredrick looked up that he saw the multiple baffles hanging from the ceiling, as well as extra foam, to absorb and break up all noise.

Interesting. He'd never seen such a configuration before. Why were the agents here allowed such luxury? Why weren't they operating under harsher conditions? Was it because this was a Yu'udir station, and they were supposed to be more bothered by noise than most races?

Stranger and stranger.

Each cubicle could be specially configured for a particular race's needs. The Yu'udir tended to have the outer ring of cubes, where additional cooling vents had been placed.

The Bantel—Riley—sat at her desk, working on a computer when he passed by. She still wore the same blue uniform, with the same unfortunate shade of light blue skin and blazing red eyes. The walls of her cubical were a uniform light gray with nothing to break up the monotony. She hadn't decorated her cubical at all, then again, supposedly she'd just transferred there.

He would have sworn that she was part of this crew, this conspiracy. And yet, why was she still here if the ship was long gone?

That afternoon, Fredrick sat on his own private courier ship digging into this Bantel's background. He actually printed out her badge photo, attaching it to the wall beside his terminal. She stared at him with soulful eyes that looked a little lost. Though all of her records and his own personal meeting with her had proved that she was as chipper as the rest of her species, there still appeared to be something a little sad or perhaps wistful in her expression.

Dig as he could, Fredrick couldn't find any seams in the Bantel's background, nothing that triggered his sense of something being off. She appeared to be exactly what she was, a Bantel who had been transferred because of some sort of issue that was merely hinted at in her record.

Was it because she was sad? There was a mention that Riley had had a brief bout of depression at one point.

Had she stolen something else? Was that why she'd been transferred? Had she just held the i-stick for a moment before convincing herself that it was wrong to steal, and so she'd returned it?

Fredrick didn't know for certain. But since the ship was gone (again), and if he was honest with himself, he really wanted to spend a bit more time away from the *Dallas* station, away from Clayton and his pervasive influence.

Instead, Fredrick decided to follow the one lead he had. He made plans to go to the *Niocia* space station, to interview Bantel's former boss.

See what misdeeds this Riley had committed. See if this really was a coincidence, or if there was a deeper conspiracy.

CHAPTER 16

BASIL

The i-stick recorder that Basil had given Kim primarily copied over what was frequently referred to as the "external" programs of an i-stick. Nothing that required a passcode or key to access. Merely the frequencies and codes used to interface with the outside world.

If they'd had more time, zie could have made a full copy of the i-stick. But that would take minutes, and Kim had only had a few seconds. What she'd transferred to the ship had been sufficient.

What people tended to forget was that i-sticks were frequently used to unlock doors as part of their public function.

Whatever doors Fredrick had access to, Basil now also had access to.

Zie wasn't sure exactly where that would take zim. Zie suspected most Cartel doors would now be open to zim and the rest of the crew. Zie was still parsing out all the codes and ascertaining exactly how high of a security clearance zie could now fake.

In the meanwhile, Basil had another role to play. The

mark had taken the bait, particularly since they'd left Kim behind on the station. That hadn't been the original plan. Originally, Kim was supposed to be able to record more of the i-stick.

That the Bantel hadn't felt comfortable keeping the i-stick after meeting the mark was telling. Kim wasn't afraid of anything. She had a certain cheerful confidence that she could get herself out of whatever trouble she ran into. Being caught stealing and made part of Arthur's program certainly hadn't changed that opinion.

Eleanor and the rest of her crew had taken off for the *Niocia* space station ahead of Fredrick. They had docked with the station using yet another ship registration, a new one that Basil had created during the past week. It wouldn't be good enough to get them off the station and through the hyper-gate. At least, not yet.

The *Niocia* space station was in a primarily Oligochuno system, one that Basil was familiar with. Not that zie had been here for a long while. There wasn't anyone here who would recognize zim. Zie still went ahead and changed zir chemical signature.

People joked about how members of a certain race (different than theirs) all looked alike. For the Oligochuno, to a certain extent, this was actually true. They didn't use merely a single sense for identifying each other or members of their clan. Their entire sensor array could be used to determine body temperature and density, chemical composition, and certainly scent.

Basil wasn't happy about rubbing a scent-changing chemical across zir entire body. It would only last for a few hours, half a day at most. But it would allow Basil to impersonate another Oligochuno completely.

Fortunately, Basil didn't need a Cartel uniform. The Oligochuno didn't wear clothing. Zie just had zir badge adhered to zir skin in the middle of zir torso, as the others did.

The *Niocia* space station was of a uniquely Oligochuno design. Instead of being a series of rings along a central spine, it was a set of spiraling tunnels that were all interconnected. Basil likened it to a series of long, tube-like bodies that had twisted around the center sphere in some sort of primitive sexual dance. The station glowed white in the distance, clean in the depths of space.

Inside, particularly in the Oligochuno areas, the air was rich and full of scents. Instead of the usual sterile air that dried out zir skin, it was humid and lush. Vines and other greenery hung from the ceiling. The walls were covered in tapestries that were not just visually striking, but were meant to be touched, tasted, and smelled. The floor was also an interesting texture to inch across, the perfect amount of grit to allow zim to grip but not too much, so it wasn't irritating. Plus, colorful mosaics were interspersed with the regular grainy floor.

Zie felt as though zie had just left a desert and was finally in a civilized area again. For some of the Oligochuno, such a constant barrage on their senses left them feeling over-whelmed.

For Basil, zie finally felt properly invigorated by zir envi-ronment.

Zie was going to spend some of zir credits to decorate zir rooms on the ship after this. Zie doubted that Judit would be thrilled with such changes in the engineering rooms. Maybe just a hanging plant or two…

The doorway to the Cartel area of the space station wasn't hidden. However, for someone who wasn't an Oligochuno, it wasn't obvious, either. Just a straight line in a section of a wall that had a lot of waves and curves covered in a textured paint that had an interesting chemical signature as well.

Zie used the i-stick that zie had modified, based on Fredrick's parameters. It let zim right into the office without a pause. Zie already had a plan. The manager that zie was impersonating had received an "urgent" message about needing to return home immediately due to an incident there.

It would take several hours for the misunderstanding—and the leaking fire suppressant—to be cleared up. At which point, Basil would be long gone.

In the meantime, zir first appointment for the day was with a Yu'udir named Fredrick.

Zie had just finished setting up in the office when the Yu'udir stuck his head in the door. He wore a Cartel blue vest and matching flat cap. While all the Yu'udir were tall, this one appeared even taller and broader than most. Menefry would have matched him for size and possibly for strength.

Basil straightened up from the resting spot that zie had adopted. Zie had three arms at that point, two for typing and a third for using the mouse or ten-digit keypad on the side.

"Come in, come in," Basil said on seeing the other person. Zie had made sure that there would be an appropriate chair on the other side of zir desk, one that would be comfortable for a Yu'udir.

Fredrick looked around the office with interest. Basil understood. At least half a dozen thriving green and red plants hung from the low ceiling. A colorful mosaic of ocean waves filled the floor with cool pebbles that Basil enjoyed inching over. Textured paint covered the walls in an abstract pattern that Basil found quite soothing, particularly using zir entire sensor array to follow along the lines and curves.

Zie understood that someone else, that is, anyone who wasn't an Oligochuno, might find the office a bit overwhelming. The colors didn't clash quite as much as, say, Kim's skin with her latest outfit. However, the harmony of the colors wouldn't be as obvious to any race whose primary sense was sight.

The office was part of why zie had chosen this manager to imitate. The Yu'udir would be distracted by everything else and not necessarily focus all of his attention on Basil.

After they'd made their introductions, Basil asked smoothly, "What can I help you with today?"

"I've just come from the *Dedmund* station. I had a run-in with one of your former employees, Riley? A Bantel?"

"Riley?" Basil asked. Zie nodded, and then pulled up a file on zir computer. "Ah, yes. I remember her. What has she stolen this time?"

Fredrick blinked, taken aback. "You know that she steals things?"

"She's really good at her job," Basil said, defending her. "She has a nose for which shipments might contain contraband. She's one of the best customs agents that I've ever worked with."

"But?" Fredrick prompted.

"But she also has sticky fingers." Basil gave a harsh imitation of a laugh. Fredrick didn't cringe, which told Basil a lot about the Yu'udir's ability to focus. "Get it? A Bantel? With those pads on their fingertips? Never mind. Yes, she sometimes can't help but steal something small from someone. However, she's had enough therapy that she always returns the item."

"Always?" Fredrick asked, obviously disapproving that any such person was allowed free rein, particularly in Cartel space.

"Always," Basil said firmly. "It took some time to condition her impulses. She can't help but steal, and trying to break those habits would have broken her, at least according to our best therapists. Instead, they focused on making sure she returns whatever she takes. So, yes, she still occasionally gets the temptation to take something. But she always gives it back."

"Why isn't she still here, working with you?" Fredrick said. He appeared truly curious.

Basil gave a heart-felt sigh. "As I said, she has a really good sense of contraband. She stole from one of those ships. I told everyone who would listen that she'd taken the cargo in order to prove that it was, in fact, contraband. However, it turned out that one of the upper managers had been involved in hushing up the smuggling. So though what she stole helped convict zim, there was too much bad blood for her to stay here."

Most of what Basil told Fredrick was actually true. Zie had merely changed a few names to place "Riley" at the heart of the investigation. Or at least that was what Fredrick would find when he started digging into the reports, most of which had never been filed officially due to the involvement of upper management.

"I see," Fredrick said. He shook his head. "So you think that Riley is harmless?"

Basil tilted zir head from side to side. "Mostly harmless. She has a good soul. And she's too useful for waste. Plus, keeping her busy and working for Universal means she has a chance to put her talents to work. If she were let go, she'd use her talents against us. And she's had bouts of depression in the past, when she wasn't fully occupied."

"Universal isn't in the business of saving people," Fredrick said slowly.

"Yes, it is," Basil said, disagreeing vehemently. "Without Universal, the entire universe would dissolve into chaos. Everyone, even Riley, needs to have a place, in order to do their part, to ensure that doesn't happen."

Fredrick gave Basil a toothy smile. "It's good to hear those sentiments coming from someone in your position."

Basil tilted zir head to the side. "I take it you're upper management?"

"Something like that," Fredrick said, waving his hand as if pushing aside the question.

They sat in awkward silence for a few moments.

"Is there anything else I can help you with?" Basil said. Zie gave a sheepish grin. "These reports won't write themselves."

Fredrick nodded slowly. "I'm looking for a ship that is using a series of different registrations. Would Riley be good with something like that?"

Basil maintained zir smile despite zir shock. This Yu'udir really *was* looking for them, specifically. They were going to have to be extra careful.

Zie finally managed to reply to Fredrick's question. "I don't know if Riley would be good finding a ship like that. Is it smuggling contraband? That's really Riley's forte."

On the one limb, getting Kim into this bastard's organization would really put them an inch or two ahead.

On the other limb, it would also expose her, placing her directly in the monster's den, as it were.

Plus, zie didn't want to appear too eager. They had a cover for Kim, and a good one. Zie would just as soon keep that cover, not blow through it.

"Of course they're smuggling. Why else would they be hiding as they are?" Fredrick said.

Basil tilted zir head from side to side again. Zie was not fooled. This Cartel minion was dangerous, and searching for something else.

"You may want to give her a trial run, see if she would fit in to your organization. I had hoped that the *Dedmund* station would be a good place for her, out of the way with a close-knit group of workers." Basil stopped and sighed. "She'd learn quickly who she could steal from, who would consider it a game, as several did here in this office. As well as who wouldn't."

"I might do that," Fredrick said. "Give her a trial run. See if I could use her particular talents."

A soft ping on Basil's computer drew zir attention. "I'm sorry," zie said. "I have another call coming in."

"Thank you for your time," Fredrick said. "This has been most enlightening."

"Thank you for being so thorough in your investigation, for not just booting Riley out," Basil said. "I take it that she stole something from you?"

"Yes," Fredrick said, showing all his teeth. "But she returned it. I was just curious why."

Basil nodded, then gestured toward zir computer again.

"Thank you," Fredrick said as he headed out the door.

Basil felt zieself trembling all up and down zir core. Despite how polite Fredrick had seemed, Basil knew that he was a killer at heart. A consummate, polite predator. No wonder Kim hadn't wanted to hold onto his i-stick for longer than she had!

Quickly, Basil scooted around the desk, snagging the i-stick reader that zie had so carefully planted on the back of the chair that Fredrick had sat in. That chime that had rung on his computer had just been the program letting zim know that the deep scan of the i-stick was complete.

Zie wouldn't have been able to do anything with an ordinary i-stick, not without that first read of the external, public properties, and time spent hacking through those.

Now, zie had a complete deep read of everything. Including all the passwords that Fredrick had probably changed immediately after his encounter with "Riley."

Basil scooted back behind the desk, making sure everything was cleared out so he could leave when someone said, "Excuse me."

It took all of zir training to not flinch at the noise, to instead slowly straighten up. Zie didn't bothering turning zir head—zir sensing array went all the way around it. "Yes?" zie inquired, seeing that Fredrick had come back.

"I have just one other question," Fredrick said, coming back into the office.

"All right?" Basil said, trying to sound nonchalant. Luckily the Yu'udir couldn't sense zir heartrate, which had skyrocketed.

"Is there a particular category of contraband that Riley is best suited for?" Fredrick asked.

The only Oligochuno who learned how to hold their mouth in a smile were those who spent a lot of time with Humans or Yu'udir. It wasn't a natural or normal expression for them.

However, for this occasion, Basil made the effort to try to smile at the Yu'udir. Zie did try to make the motion look awkward, as if it wasn't something that zie did on a regular basis.

"I'm glad you asked! Yes, there is. She's very knowledgeable about artwork and stolen antiquities. While she might get lucky on a narcotics case, she's much more attuned with artwork," Basil said. Zie dropped the smile. "Why do you ask?"

"I wanted to make sure that I pointed her in the right direction," Fredrick said smoothly. "Okay, I'll get out of your fur now."

Basil didn't point out that zie had no fur, or even hair.

This time, Basil stayed at zir desk, tracking Fredrick, making sure the Yu'udir had actually left the Cartel office area before zie, too, inched away.

Zie was afraid that zie might have put Kim into the monster's den. But surely she'd be able to handle it, right?

CHAPTER 17

MENEFRY

IT HAD TAKEN SOME DOING, BUT MENEFRY HAD FINALLY convinced the others to allow Dale to come aboard *Eleanor* as a passenger. They were going to have to work to make sure that the Bantel didn't have access to the secondary engineering room. There was nothing in the primary room that would indicate the existence of the secondary.

The ability to be able to transform the ship, to hide convincingly against the stars and blackness, was worth it. It would give them so much of an edge over the Cartel.

And keep them safe.

Judit had complained (of course) about the contract she was going to have to write up. Basil had said that zie would work with Eleanor to ensure that the doors of the ship were properly coded so that only the crew could access them. Eleanor would also be able to track Dale at all times. Should the Bantel disappear from her sensors, she'd automatically lock down wherever he'd been most recently, trapping him until he reappeared again.

Saxon hadn't said much. Then again, Saxon hadn't said much of anything since returning from Yau'Mrapa. Menefry wasn't certain what had gone on, though he suspected that the aspect of the Goddess for Calming Fighting Families would be appropriate (one hand raised, one foot in front of the other, the rest of her limbs soft and welcoming).

On the trip back from *Niocia* to *Dedmund*, Menefry worked with Eleanor, developing an interface that would allow the ship access to the cloaking device, based on a prototype that Dale had given him.

Menefry was working in his "office," the desert conference room. Basil had managed to hack into the programming of the hologram walls so that instead of a sunset every hour, it was only once every four hours.

Every time the sun set, Menefry would stop what he was doing and give thanks to the Goddess.

This meant he was praying more often than usual, as generally he prayed when he rose, at noon, and in the evening. However, he also felt as if the ship and the crew needed more blessings from the Goddess than most.

At Judit's request, Menefry didn't burn incense in here, though he had added a small statue of the Goddess, maybe fifteen centimeters tall and carved out of black stone. She stood high on a shelf in the corner, holding the pose of Sage Counsel with the top two limbs raised up to channel golden light down onto the proceedings, the middle sets of hands pressed together in prayer, and the bottom limbs exaggerated, almost touching the shelf she sat on, grounding everyone. Even Kim had approved of the fuchsia-colored gauze wrapped around the torso of the statue.

Normally, the warmth of the office made Menefry feel more comfortable. The sight of the desert surrounding him reminded him of home. He could hear the soft shifting of the sand, almost smell the baked rocks. He'd also slightly increased the gravity here, just to help him feel more grounded.

However, all of that felt oppressive that afternoon. There was a burden pressing down on his shell that he couldn't place.

Eleanor had just finished giving him feedback on the latest prototype interface that Menefry had connected together, making a few tweaks on the back end so that when they got back to *Balmor* station, it would be easy to connect up the grid of wires that they could use for a cloaking device.

"Thank you," Menefry told Eleanor, adjusting a few more things on his side before pushing his kneeling chair back and away. He sat for a few moments, contemplating the amber spire in front of him, the holographic representation that Eleanor used when speaking with the crew.

"What is it?" Eleanor asked after a few moments. She gave a soft chuckle. "Or do you have the same doubts that Judit has, and are afraid that we're due for more bad luck?"

Menefry tilted his head from one side to the other. "Bad luck, just like good luck, is the will of the Goddess," he said. And while he believed that, he was also not fatalistic about it, not like some of the orthodox who preached that you should just accept whatever fate was handed to you.

Seemed that those who were the luckiest also generally worked the hardest.

No, there was something else, just outside the reach of his mandibles, that he couldn't quite snag.

"What do the others think about the cloaking device?" he found himself asking.

"The rest of the crew?" Eleanor said.

Menefry blinked and reconsidered his question. "No," he said slowly. "Gawain and Abban."

"They…don't wish to be involved," Eleanor said after a moment.

"Why not?" Menefry said, his head tilting to one side.

While on the one limb, Eleanor was generally the one who interacted with the crew.

On the other limb, now that he thought about it, he hadn't heard from the other two in a while.

"Are they all right?" Menefry said. He remembered Judit's fears that the three Chonchu, cut off for so long from their queens, might eventually start going insane.

"They're fine," Eleanor assured him. "They're just… working on other things."

"Such as?" Menefry asked. That niggling feeling at the back of his shell had just doubled in size and weight.

"They're both working on the engines right now," Eleanor said after a moment.

"Without you?" Menefry said softly.

The sigh Eleanor gave sounded as if floating on the winds of the Goddess. It struck his heart deeply, as it carried with it such pain and loneliness.

"I run the exterior," Eleanor said. "I have you, the crew. The other two, they don't interact with you as much. So they've turned further inward."

"Are you worried?" Menefry said. She certainly sounded worried.

A few moments passed. Would she answer the question?

"Yes," came the whispered reply.

"How can we help?" Menefry said. "Should I try to ask them about these designs?"

"It won't do any good," Eleanor said. "They need…they need more."

"And what would more involve?" Menefry said, afraid of what the answer might be.

"Nothing that we want to try yet," Eleanor said, sounding determined. "Please, don't tell Judit about this. Not at this point. Let me try working with them some more."

"All right," Menefry said, nodding slowly. "I'll not tell the rest of the crew. But you have to keep me informed about how far they're withdrawing. We need them."

Eleanor gave a soft laugh. "I know. We all need them. I'll keep talking with them, trying to bring their focus back out."

The amber spire of Eleanor dissolved gracefully, the golden motes dancing for a few moments before it was gone.

Menefry felt the weight of his worry return. There was something wrong with the beings who were, in essence, the secondary engines.

If something went really amiss with them, the ship would no longer be functional. If they managed to fall out of hyperspace without imploding, chances were, they'd be facing a long run from wherever they ended up back to civilization. And they just weren't set up for that.

Menefry decided to add more supplies the next time they reached a station. Some emergency rations, enough to get the entire crew through a couple of months without resupplying themselves. Give them at least a chance of surviving.

For now, he looked up at the small statue of the Goddess, then stepped off his chair and carefully lowered himself onto his back. They were always in her limbs, may they be ever weaving. Hopefully, his prayers would bring them some of the wise counsel they needed at this junction.

Because he had the feeling that their run of bad luck was just beginning.

CHAPTER 18

KIM

Kim finished her letter with a small smiley face at the bottom.

How else were you supposed to close a suicide note?

She wasn't angry that her friends had abandoned her on the *Dedmund* station. She understood why it was that they'd needed to leave, to continue with the plan.

But now, Fredrick was back. And he was hunting her. He'd already sent her a message that she was supposed to go to his office in the morning. He was in the process of getting her reassigned to his "team."

He was going to find something in her cover that wasn't right. Some chink in the electronic armor that Basil had built.

Then Fredrick was going to put her in a locked room, like what she'd been trapped in on the *Gery* station. With a monster hiding in the dark behind her, just waiting to snap her head off with a single bite.

Kim kept all her biological readings depressed. Anyone viewing the readouts would see that while her heartrate might be high, all her other readings were low. She took shallow breaths through her mouth, deliberately eschewing the happy oxygen that might bring her more cheer.

Slowly, Kim rose from her desk. It was really just a matter of time. She had to get out, *now*, before Fredrick's minions came to pick her up, throw her in prison.

Because this time, Judit's tricks wouldn't work. They wouldn't be able to rescue her. Had they ever planned to in the first place? Or had they left her behind on purpose, a sacrificial lamb?

Just thinking about it made tears come to Kim's eyes. It was one of the few traits that the Bantel shared with the Humans and the Yu'udir. She blinked her eyes, trying to hold them back.

One shaky sob, then she shook herself. No, no one outside of her small nest was going to see her cry.

With a nod to the brightly colored walls, pillows, and blankets that had cheered up her room on the *Dedmund* station, Kim walked out the door, her head held high.

She went in a roundabout way to the outer edge of the space station. She didn't move too fast or too slow. Everything was normal here, see? She was just meandering through the station. Learning her way around. She was new here, right?

No one would see how deliberate her course was until after.

After…

Kim found her footsteps slowing as she approached the airlock. She'd identified it earlier, as it was one with the fewest safety controls that were actually working. Seemed that the maintenance in this area wasn't as precise as it had been in some of the other parts of the station.

Perhaps this was one of the places that smugglers used, to get goods on and off the station.

But it meant that no automatic system was going to

check and see if she was actually wearing a space suit when she opened the outer hatch.

Kim looked down at her current outfit. It was cute, of course. Kim didn't do plain. But it was more subdued than her usual choices. The blues all matched the Cartel uniforms she was surrounded with every day. Her skin, too, was a nice complementary blue. Instead of blazing red with rage, her eyes were golden, shining with the wisdom she'd gathered up these last few days.

All right, so maybe the blues were a bit on point when it came to her depression. But she couldn't help it! It was the best she could do on short notice.

No one was around. The ubiquitous station cameras were conspicuously absent in this hallway.

Taking one last breath of freedom, Kim opened the airlock door, stepping into the small chamber beyond.

Of course, the stupid windows both looking into the chamber and out onto space were far above her head. This was a Yu'udir station, and they hadn't thought to build something that a Bantel could use.

That was all right. No one had to see her now.

Kim punched in the security code to open the outer doors. The ones that would flood the small chamber with the vacuum of space.

She let a single tear slowly glide down her face as she waited for the countdown, the alarms blasting, making sure that people knew that certain death was coming if they weren't prepared.

Kim touched the edge of the door, as if for good luck. She nodded once.

Then the outer doors opened, and her body was flung out into the emptiness beyond.

CHAPTER 19

JUDIT

JUDIT STOOD WITH BASIL AT THE BACK OF THE PRIMARY engine room, in front of the airlock. The two huge engine tubes on either side of the large, echoing space hummed softly, a sound that Judit never took for granted. She'd found herself getting so jumpy when she'd gone down to Yau'Mrapa with Saxon. It was just too damned quiet on a planet. No way of telling if you were flying right or not.

Basil's second office crouched in one of the far corners, temporary walls giving it shape. At least zie had finished whatever obnoxious experiment that zie had been conducting, and the worst of the smell had been vented away.

Seemed that the best way for a biological-based ship to take care of itself was to feed it certain nutrients to get it to grow and make repairs.

It was an elegant enough solution, though it bothered Judit that more and more of the control of the ship was being turned over to the beings running the ship. While Basil had dismantled most of the "leashes" that Masala had originally installed, zie had maintained a few, mainly at Judit's request.

She didn't trust turning all control of the ship over to any one being, even if the Chonchu at the heart of the ship were actually three beings and not an artificial intelligence.

At least the trip back to the *Dedmund* station had been uneventful.

A long, extendable arm, attached to the outside of *Eleanor*, had reached its full capacity and was slowly being reeled back, the end of it firmly wrapped around its payload.

The pair of them patiently waited as the airlock slowly cycled, forcing the vacuum of space out and bringing the chamber up to pressure and gravity.

Finally, the airlock finished cycling and Kim stepped through. She carried her EVA helmet under one arm. The suit was covered in wires, the technology that Dale had invented.

With just a flick of a switch, Kim appeared to be dressed in plain blue clothes, not wearing any outer protective layer.

"Hi ya!" Kim said as she stepped across the threshold and onto the ship.

"Welcome aboard," Judit said. "I take it there was no problem?"

"Nope, none!" Kim said cheerily. "Though it was kinda hard, you know? To pretend to be so sad. But I did it. I think I convinced everyone! I even convinced myself for a while, you know?"

Basil nodded. "Your personnel records already showed that you were prone to bouts of depression. And I may have hinted at that to Fredrick as well."

Kim beamed at them. Judit had to work hard to not roll her eyes. She might pull something if she did.

Hopefully, "Riley's" suicide would move Fredrick's attention away from the Bantel. They'd left the *Niocia* with a new ship registration, one that shouldn't be on Fredrick's list. Basil had been able to acquire a new identity during zir time acting as a Cartel manager at the station.

It wasn't quite time for the hunted to become the hunters. There were a few more things that needed to be set into place.

But soon, *very* soon, Judit was finally going to be able to stop being chased and start chasing.

And at that point, the entire Cartel had better beware.

———

Judit almost, *almost* felt good about going back to *Balmor* station. On the one hand, no one knew their ship's registration. They were finally safe enough to go to stations and not have to worry about being tracked.

On the other hand, they *had* been there before. They were specifically going back to see if they could get a new contract with NEL. She was going to have to explain the ship's new registry, though as Saxon had pointed out, she could just pretend it was a brand-new ship as no one from the company had ever seen it or been onboard.

Judit also worried about Saxon. He'd been withdrawn since his brother's death, along with his sister's refusal to see the truth of his chosen isolation from the rest of his family. She understood that at some point he could go back home; Flora wouldn't forbid it. However, the whole situation stunk.

She was glad that she'd decided it was best for everyone back home to just believe she was dead. She had no desire to play the part of the prodigal daughter, returning home.

No, home was always where she made it. And right now, that was on *Eleanor*. Even if sometimes it felt more like a trap, like a long run, than a home.

The approach to the *Balmor* space station had been normal. She'd left a message with Tess, her contact at NEL, letting her know that they'd like another chance at a contract.

However, Tess hadn't sent a reply.

That was unusual. Judit had met with Tess a few times. She was Human, with short brassy curls and solid muscles. Like Judit, someone might mistakenly assume that Tess was overweight, though she could probably bench press Saxon.

Tess was so no-nonsense she made Judit look fanciful by comparison.

After they'd docked inside the station, paying extra for that berth so that Menefry could work with Dale to encase *Eleanor* in hidden wires, Judit decided to pay a trip to the NEL headquarters.

If they were going to refuse her offer of flying for them, they were going to have to do it to her face.

The Human sector of the space station was as bland as the Bantel side. Industrial gray paint covered any wear and tear that the walls or floor might have suffered. The Humans appeared just as non-descript, wearing shades of beige, brown, and black pants and shirts.

More than one Human culture was represented on the station. Not Hungarian, of course. They were too small to make their presence known. But she passed more than one curry house that had her mouth watering, along with a few dumpling and dim sum places.

Maybe she'd have to stop at one of those on her way back to the ship.

And yet, even the small restaurants weren't decorated. A few had large painted signs in front of their shops, but most just blended into the background.

Was that because this was a spy station? No one wanted to stand out, to be memorable?

That was stupid. It made Judit want to turn around and change her clothes, change out of her dark maroon shirt and black pants. Maybe she could borrow something from Kim's closet, just to make a splash.

Except that she and the rest of the crew actually *didn't*

want to stand out either. They wanted to pass through here like ghosts and be gone, with no one the wiser.

It grated on Judit's nerves, but she had to accept that was where they stood at this time.

Judit left the main marketplace and headed outward, toward the curve of the station, where another very large spaceport was located. The offices for NEL were located near there, along with dozens of other transport companies, most of which were merely fronts for the Cartel.

Unlike on a planet, where each building was separate from its neighbors, on a space station, everything was sensibly run together. Offices were located behind separate doors of a long row of buildings. There wasn't that much to distinguish between them beyond the signs out front. A few had gone the extra kilometer and actually painted the outside of their office, generally the colors of their logo.

While the bright yellow of one was memorable, only a Bantel would have approved. The brown and green one was probably supposed to look lush, though it reminded her of moldy stew.

NEL's headquarters were a nice comforting gray, though she did appreciate the red racing stripes that had been added around the front window and door.

However, the windows were dark. The red neon "Open" sign was turned off. The office felt abandoned.

Judit paused for a moment. Had there been a power outage in this section? Nope. Windows were lit in the building on either side. Just the NEL headquarters were dark.

She hesitated, but still made herself walk forward and try the door.

Locked.

Mi a pokol?

Were they just closed for the day? Had there been some trouble? What was going on? *Eleanor* and her crew had only been gone from the *Balmor* station for fourteen—maybe fifteen—days. Surely they hadn't gone out of business.

Judit left the warehouses and went back to the market-place, getting herself a lovely eggplant curry dish that she carried to one of the back corners of a restaurant. As it was more than an hour before what would be the common lunch time on the station, only a few of the other dozen or so tables were filled, all with Humans of various races. Soft music played in the background, the singer obviously bemoaning something: a hangnail, a torn shirt, a broken heart. It all sounded the same to her.

Once Judit was ensconced at her table, she pulled out her i-stick and plugged into the local network, scrolling through the news.

It appeared that the chief logistics officer for NEL had been lured to a different company, obviously a Cartel front, the week before *Eleanor* had arrived at *Balmor* the first time.

Bad debts that the company had were suddenly exposed, the day Judit and the others had left the station. Other troubles had started. Ships had stopped working for NEL. The company had had to pay out huge fines as deliveries were late.

Their margins had always been razor thin. The company hadn't died from a single blow, but a thousand cuts that all happened at the same time, over the matter of a couple of weeks.

Instead of trying to delay the death, they'd pulled the plug abruptly, just the day before.

It seemed like coincidence. However, it wasn't. Judit could tell, could see the pattern that it actually made.

Someone in the Cartel—Fredrick?—had made that offer to the chief logistics officer. As well as nudged along some of the other factors. Possibly had bribed a couple of ships to be late with their cargo, so that NEL had to pay out.

It stank to *menny* and back.

Judit slowly ate her curry, dunking her naan into the dregs of the sauce to finish it off.

She'd heard of this sort of consolidation before. The Cartel would drain off resources from an independent organization just so that they could be the only major player left.

How many of the remaining independent cargo shipping companies would still be in business by the end of next year? How many of them would be swallowed? So many of the existing companies were already merely fronts for the Cartel.

Judit sighed deeply into her empty bowl. It made her want to find whatever part of the station was considered the "bad" side, just so she could start something.

She hadn't been in a bar fight for ages…

However, she couldn't afford to get arrested, or brought before any port authorities. She was just going to have to take her aggression out on the punching bag back at the ship.

Then, after she'd worked off some of her anger issues, she was going to have to find them a new shipping contract. And company. And hope that they could somehow start turning a profit again.

Soon.

CHAPTER 20

BASIL

Basil was a little disappointed by what zie found zie could access using Fredrick's i-stick.

Turned out, not a lot.

Basil wasn't interested in the Yu'udir's bank accounts or credit line. Touching those would be the fastest way to getting caught. The passwords stored in the i-stick had already gotten zim into some of the more secure Cartel systems, and zie appreciated those.

However, that was about it. Seemed that Fredrick didn't trust online storage systems for his data. There weren't a lot of files that Basil could access, and what zie did access were pretty mundane.

The most interesting thing about Fredrick's i-stick was the search history, what Fredrick had been looking for in public databases.

Probably the more interesting searches had been done on his master's computers, and all traces of those would be carefully expunged on a regular basis, no matter what sort of recordkeeping the law required.

The Cartel was always above all those sorts of legal niceties.

Basil worked at the computer system in the primary engineering room. Zie had added two hanging plants to the area, one in the primary engineering room and one in the secondary. Eleanor had seemed bemused by the greenery, but hadn't objected. Each pot was about thirty centimeters deep and across, hanging by metal chains.

It was the one bright spot in the room, and Basil found zir eyes drawn to it frequently.

The leaves were round, thick, and shiny, with a chemical signature that Basil found pleasing. They were mottled green, white, and yellow, and grew along thin vines just starting to trail over the edges of the white pot that held them. A mesh was attached to the top of the pot, meant to keep the dirt in place in case of a sudden loss of gravity. Even though the pot was a couple of meters away, Basil could still occasionally catch a whiff of the rich soil and growing vegetation.

Zie had set up a timer to remember to water the plants. They both appeared to be thriving in the existing lights, the shopkeeper having assured zim that they wouldn't need any special spectrum.

At some point, zie would like to hang more plants overhead. Possibly even repaint the floor. While the thick black rubber had the perfect amount of grip for zim, it was still so staid. Nothing interesting about inching over it. Zie had gotten spoiled at the *Niocia* station and all those mosaics swirling across the floors.

With a sigh, Basil returned zir attention to the computer screen. Zie had three arms that day, as zie had had when pretending to be a Cartel manager, two for typing and one for the key pad.

Fredrick had been searching a series of companies. While

the Yu'udir had found over a dozen in some of his initial searches, his interest had focused in on four.

Basil found it interesting that all four had been created a few months ago. When zie checked the dates, zie realized their creation had occurred just two weeks before *Camelot* had been destroyed. A large amount of credits had been transferred into these companies one week after they'd been formed.

Then, two days after the tragedy, a tremendous number of credits had been funneled through the companies.

Where had the money come from?

It turned out to be from a myriad of smaller companies, all of which had been in existence for quite a few years.

Looking over the decades, Basil could see a distinct pattern, how those companies went almost dormant for a while, then there would be a flurry of activity, followed by near dormancy again.

Zie tried peeling back the layers of the onion on that side. However, whoever had set up the originating companies had done too good of a job. Zie wasn't getting anywhere pursuing those. It would take an actual forensic accountant, one who was a natural predator, and even then the outcome wasn't assured.

The receiving companies, though, were fairly easy to pull apart. Whoever had done the work was an amateur. It didn't take that much effort, now that zie knew where to look, to reveal that yes, they had all been set up by a shell corporation.

A name came up. One that zie had seen before.

Sachiko.

Those companies were all based around her. And all those credits had probably been funneled to her as well.

It was enough money to buy a space station outright. Smaller than *Camelot,* though not by much.

Had it been payment for blowing it up?

Basil didn't know for certain. However, zie had a feeling in zir gut about this. Or the Oligochuno equivalent—all of zir segments lined up just so.

Was this enough to bring to Judit and the others? Possibly. Zie would certainly spell it out in zir next report.

It was such a shame that no one else felt the need to write up reports like zie did. They always seemed to feel that just meeting and talking about it would be enough. Basil was the only one who came to any of their meetings with reports actually finished.

Zie contained zir sigh.

In the meantime, zie turned zir attention back to the next experiment that zie needed to run. The chemicals that zie had introduced had appeared to be the right ones, and the pipe that zie had originally removed from the secondary engine was in the process of growing back.

Now, to see if zie could improve them. Eleanor claimed that Gawain and Abban weren't feeling one hundred percent since Basil had changed their formula. They'd been so quiet lately.

It was something else that left zir segments unsettled. That sense that something was wrong with the ship, though Eleanor assured zim that zie was getting as paranoid as Judit.

Was zie? Or was Eleanor lying to him?

CHAPTER 21

MENEFRY

Menefry didn't get a response to the inquiry he sent to Dale. He didn't worry, though. Dale had been unresponsive before. The Bantel would get so involved in whatever project he was working on that he wouldn't hear his terminal chime, wouldn't feel his i-stick vibrate, and wouldn't raise his head back up for a couple of days.

Still, Menefry had good news for the Bantel, so he decided to go back out to Dale's warehouse, to give him the news in person.

The Bantel section of the *Balmor* space station was still built for all aliens, so while Menefry could fit through the corridors and walk through the hallways without having to crouch or bend his head down, they were still smaller and more tightly packed. He felt hemmed in as he walked. He wore synthetic trousers the color of the blessed night sky, along with a loose dark-brown vest, both of which were made of a heavier material, meant to keep a Khanvassa warm.

He had changed the location of his i-stick, moving it from a lower pocket to higher, attached to his collar. Anyone trying to steal it would have a difficult time, mainly because it was now located far above the heads of those he passed.

Carrying beamers or other sorts of particle weapons wasn't allowed on *Balmor* station. However, people could still wear knives and such. Menefry made sure to have at least two visible knives tucked into a belt around his waist, and if someone was paying attention, they might also see a couple more sticking out of the tops of his boots.

He carried other weapons as well, just not as visibly.

This meant that while the corridors he passed through were crowded, no one bothered him. It was just his imagination that he sometimes felt the feather-light touch of fingers on his empty pockets.

Though you could never be too paranoid…

The warehouse section looked the same as it had, most of the buildings plain gray with no windows, while the artists cooperative was brightly painted with many windows.

Dale's name was still in the directory for the building, and when Menefry typed in the code, the door was buzzed open immediately.

However, it wasn't Dale who opened the door to the workshop. No, it was a completely different Bantel.

The new Bantel weighed quite a bit more than Dale, who'd always struck Menefry as being on the skinny side. This Bantel's eyes were smaller as well, and his nose was quite a bit bigger. He wore a gray-and-white boxed pattern on his shirt. It wasn't plaid, as the boxes were irregular and at odd angles. Kim would turn her nose up at the plain colors, despite the interesting pattern. The pants the Bantel wore were almost identical to Menefry's, a solid black that looked warm.

His skin was a golden color, with searing red eyes. He appeared to be glaring at Menefry, though it was difficult to tell with the color and all. Unlike most of the Bantel Menefry had met, this one seemed dour.

Maybe it was just the place, and Menefry had been expecting melancholy.

"Yeah?" the Bantel asked, standing in the doorway.

"I'm here to see Dale," Menefry said. He looked over the head of the Bantel, into the workroom.

The large worktable still stood in the center of the place. However, instead of racks holding fabric and clothing lining the walls, metal sculptures crowded the space. A flower motif was repeated over and over again: a small base, maybe thirty centimeters square, from which rose a plain metal rod. A large flat flower grew from the top of that, maybe twenty centimeters across the petals. The flowers were made from a shiny metal and decorated with different colored glass balls, some of which were rounded, others had been flattened out.

They weren't beautiful. Even the Goddess would have a difficult time blessing them.

"Dale's not here," the Bantel said.

"Where did he go?" Menefry asked. "What happened to him?"

"He found passage on a ship outta here," the Bantel said. "Said since he'd paid rent on the workshop through the end of the year, that I could have it."

He sounded defensive.

"I'm not here to collect rent," Menefry assured him. "I'd just thought…Did Dale leave anything for me?"

The Bantel stepped back and looked up at Menefry's face. "Oh. You're a Khanvassa, right?"

"Yes," Menefry said. Wasn't that obvious? Wouldn't that have been obvious from the moment the Bantel had opened the door?

"Yeah. That's right. Dale left something for you," the

Bantel said. "Just a second. Come on in. I'm Mel, by the way."

Menefry stepped into the workshop carefully. To his left stood a second workbench, where Mel had been carefully soldering the marbles and other glass pieces into yet another ugly flowerhead.

"Here," Mel said, coming back from the far corner of the shop with a bag that he thrust at Menefry. It was a shopping bag from the local bakery.

Inside lay the drone that Dale had demonstrated his materials on, along with what looked like a large bolt of the cloth and maybe some additional circuitry.

"Thank you," Menefry said. He glanced around the workshop again, knowing that the Goddess had just closed this path to them.

"Wanna buy a flower?" Mel asked after a moment.

"No, no thank you," Menefry said. He just barely managed to control his shudder. The only representational artwork that the Khanvassa enjoyed were statues of the Goddess. He wasn't orthodox enough to believe that anything else was blasphemy.

The flowers really were hideous.

"Good luck," Menefry said after a few more moments, before he turned and left the workshop.

NEL was gone. So was Dale. Had he found work? Or had he used his special wire on a different ship? Probably he'd just found something else.

Menefry was going to spend the rest of the afternoon searching out what exactly had happened to Dale.

Then try to come up with a plan B for how to protect his ship and his crew.

CHAPTER 22

FREDRICK

Fredrick tried to pay attention as Clayton introduced him to the other guests of the Universal dinner party they were attending.

Not as a peer. No, of course not. However, not as a minion either. If anything, Fredrick would describe his position as Clayton's "plus one" no matter how ridiculous that might sound.

This party was exactly the sort of thing that Fredrick had been scheming for, eventually. To familiarize himself with this inner circle of the true movers and shakers of the Cartel. To have an in, a way of contacting them again later.

However, he found his thoughts wandering. Particularly when one of the board members, a Bantel, came up and greeted Clayton warmly.

It was just his imagination that she was related to Riley, somehow, coincidence that her eyes were spaced about the same distance apart and that she had a smaller neck ruff, like the Bantel who'd killed herself rather than work with Fredrick.

He shook himself mentally and managed to give the person a warm, friendly smile when she introduced herself as Blair.

Her air gave her away as someone who wasn't actually related to Riley, no, this Blair seemed far too chipper and sociable. Fredrick had backed up the recording of Riley, following her into the café, watching her eat by herself. He had managed to find one other encounter of her, interacting with a couple of other customs workers. There was no sound, and with the Bantel it was almost impossible to read their lips.

However, the body language had been clear. While Riley had tried to make friends with them, they weren't interested in returning the favor. She'd left, her head down, her shoulders slumped, defeated. A few steps later, her head had come back up and a determined smile could be seen.

She wasn't going to let them get her down.

No, it was him. His summons that had done it. She'd been doing the best she could, but she couldn't face going into the monster's lair.

Fredrick still regretted his haste. Why had he pursued her? He should have kept his focus on the ship, or the shipping company, or a myriad of other projects.

Still, he couldn't show any of what he was feeling. Luckily, he was used to that, to bottling up his true emotions and never letting anything show on his face.

The dining room was supposedly elegant, with its toned-down golden-beige walls and thick carpet. All the doors were covered over with a white gauze, as if to bring an intimacy or softness to the gathering, but really, they were just an annoyance to the waitstaff. A large oval table dominated the space, covered in a heavy white linen cloth, weighed down with equally clunky cutlery and plates.

The only true color in the room was the sophisticated

glass chandelier hanging above the table. A soft green color filled the elegant tubes that flowed from the center of the piece to the arms—a type of algae used to improve air quality.

It was an expensive extravagance to have in such a small room. These sorts of glassworks were meant to clean the air for much larger spaces and generally hung in large ballrooms.

Of course, Universal always got the best for itself, never mind the expense or the waste.

Fredrick found it odd, how proud Clayton sounded when he introduced Fredrick to a Human woman, Malina. She wore an outfit that Fredrick was barely familiar with, something called a *sari*. She had a tight, neon-blue top that exposed her flat stomach, then was swathed in layers of blue and white gauzy cloth. Gold and silver dots had been stuck to her forehead in a bizarre arrangement that surely wasn't defensive or practical. A gold ring was attached to one nostril, with a chain that hung across her cheek to her ear that would be such an impediment if she was ever in a fight. Though her light brown skin showed no obvious signs of aging, her eyes were a faded color, no longer bright, though they still shone with avarice. She'd obviously tried to overcome those signs of age with the brightest red lipstick she could find, in a color that even a Bantel would approve of.

"Malina is one of the best advisors you could ask for," Clayton said. "I always listen to her wisdom."

Interesting how Malina rolled her eyes at that. "You only like me because I'm practical, dear," she teased. "And because I put profits over people."

"Exactly!" Clayton said with cheer that was clearly forced. "As I said. Practical."

They started talking about a joint venture that they'd been running.

Normally, Fredrick would have been fascinated, or at the

very least, taking mental notes so that he could track more of Clayton's business.

However, the words bantered about merely stuck to his fur and weren't combing out easily.

Of course, Universal was all about profit over people. They paid lip service to how important the people in the organization were.

People were fungible, though. The Cartel was truly all that mattered.

Fredrick had always been aware of this. He'd certainly followed along those same ruthless channels in order to further his career.

Right now, though, he was feeling less certain of his choices.

How many others had died, frozen out by those deliberate choices made by the organization? For the health of the organization?

How many other lives had Fredrick and the rest ruined in their quest for profit?

Fredrick continued to talk with those gathered around the table, speaking of profits and explaining points of business. He didn't talk about the data stream that he longed to set up, to be surrounded by pure streams of numbers and phrases. That was far too personal of a topic.

He did talk about random coincidences, and how they should be given more attention. The one Oligochuno who attended the dinner, Rosemary (who insisted on drinking something that looked like a neon-pink gelatinous material that continued to jiggle after zie set it down) was the only one who took Fredrick up on his idea, wondering how they could program for that better in their watchdog systems.

By the end of the evening, Fredrick felt as though he had a much better understanding of the circles that Clayton ran in, along with his own path.

He'd made a mistake, pushing Riley as he had.

He hadn't made a mistake coming to work for Clayton.

Or deciding that when this was all done, that he should expose all of that Human's sins for the universe to see.

CHAPTER 23

SAXON

Saxon tried not to let the morass of sorrow drown him. Judit still needed him, though she'd been good about not pushing him to work when he really wasn't ready to. The rest of the crew had been as well.

There were times when Saxon wished that someone would do, well, *something*, to get him motivated again. He was no longer spending his time reading lugubrious poetry in his chambers, roaring at the walls about the unfairness of it all.

Instead, he stared at nothing, cushioned in one of the two off-white chairs that were starting to show signs of wear. The tiny spear that he kept as a memento still stood on a small table in the corner that held his electronic reader along with a few actual volumes of poetry. His favorite flatcap—made from a brown tweed, of course—hung in the corner. He'd even found a cheap tourist memento of *Camelot*, a replica of the space station, made of plastic and painted gold. It had a place of honor hanging from the wall. He'd turned down Menefry's generous offer of a small statue of the Goddess, knowing that wouldn't actually comfort him despite the Khanvassa's insistence that the pose of Healing Suffering would help.

Saxon shifted in his chair. He'd been sitting too long. He wasn't stiff and sore, not yet. But he would be if he didn't start putting in more time in the tiny gym onboard the vessel.

The Yu'udir could be fairly inactive for long periods of time before causing active harm to themselves. That had been enforced by the long winters, when there was little to do outside, followed by furiously paced summers when there was too much to do.

At least Saxon hadn't given into his worst impulses and filled the fridge in his galley kitchen with alcoholic beverages. Sometimes he regretted that decision, though most days he understood what a bad idea that would have been.

Still, he couldn't help but start when Eleanor's warm voice spoke to him.

"Saxon?" she inquired. "Are you busy?"

"No," Saxon said sourly. He gestured to the empty space around him. There wasn't anything here for him to do. If she was peeking into his chambers, she could see that.

He did have things that he could be doing. For example, they were in the middle of a hyperspace run. He could be in the main helm with Judit.

But he'd decided to sit this short run out. Judit had found them another contract, off the *Balmor* station to another system. They wouldn't make much profit on it, but any credits coming in were good at this point.

"I…we need your help," Eleanor said after a few more moments.

"Is there something wrong with the ship?" Saxon asked. Surely Basil would be better for fixing that.

"No," Eleanor said.

Saxon wondered at her continued hesitance.

"It's Abban. And Gawain," she confessed.

"What's wrong with them?" Saxon said, sitting up from his chair, the fur across his hackles rising.

"They're not responding to me," she said quietly. "I can no longer get them to talk with me."

That was bad. That was very bad indeed.

They were in the middle of a hyperspace tunnel. If the engines stopped working, they'd "fall" out of the tunnel and implode. Even if they managed to get out safely, without the hyperspace engines they'd be facing a long run back to known space.

Possibly an incredibly long run, one measured in life-times, that would eventually kill them all.

"What can I do to help?" Saxon asked. "And why me?" He wasn't the ship's wrangler. Why wasn't she asking Basil?

"Gawain likes you," Eleanor said all in a rush. "You were the first person of the crew that he felt comfortable talking to. And Abban likes you as well. Basil's *my* contact. As is Judit."

"I see," Saxon said, though he didn't. Not really. "What would you like for me to talk to them about?"

"Grief."

———

SAXON STOOD ALONE IN HIS ROOM. HE HELD ONE OF the ancient sagas of his people in front of him, reciting the words of one of the powerful poems, the elegy to the slain. For the most part, he could recite the words from memory.

The elegy had been written down millennia ago. Supposedly it commemorated a true event, the battle between two great clans that was ended by a huge, fierce storm that had wiped out most of the survivors. The only ones who'd lived had been the ones who had worked together at the end, regardless of their clan of origin. It was an elegant reflection on not only the purpose of life, but the true meaning of conflict.

It sounded better in the original Yu'udir, but it was still a formidable piece in Common. Saxon knew that he had an elegant speaking voice, and that he gave a good recitation of the piece.

Nothing that he'd tried so far had brought out a peep from either Abban or Gawain.

Eleanor admitted that they were possibly depressed, upset that they'd been cut off from their queens and the rest of their kind for so long. She had Judit and Basil, even Menefry and Kim, who she could connect to.

Abban and Gawain felt as though they only had each other, and that wasn't enough. They needed more contact, and they'd pulled away from Eleanor.

Going back to one of the Chonchu systems was risky at best, and quite possibly deadly. There was no telling what the queens might do when faced with three of the Chonchu who had changed and evolved so far away from the others.

They might instantly be absorbed back into the Hive with no autonomy left, and the ship would crash without its brains. One of the queens might take over the ship and crash it. Or she might kill the three Chonchu instantly, assuming that they were now aliens and could no longer be accepted as part of the Hive.

Saxon had tried at first to merely talk with the two of them. When that elicited no response, he'd decided to read the poem to them.

When he finished reading, he sat down heavily in his chair, emotionally drained.

"What does it mean?" came the soft, neutral voice of Abban. "The golden fields?"

Saxon wasn't sure if he felt more relief or dread at Abban's question. On the one claw, it was good that he'd finally been able to elicit a response. Bad that the person had focused on the part of the elegy about what happened after death.

"My people believe, believed, that when your soul dies, it goes to the hall of the dead, overseen by Aredhros, the god of the dead. After many trials, those who succeed are allowed to leave the hall through the back door which leads to the fields of gold, where a person might live forever in peace and harmony."

"What do you believe?" Abban asked.

Saxon shrugged. "I don't know what will happen once my soul leaves my flesh." He paused. "There might be fields of gold. There might be nothing, and my soul will just disintegrate into motes of dust, dancing between the stars."

"We believe that you get reborn, eventually," Gawain said, suddenly joining the conversation. "Your soul is not a single piece, but is made up of many parts. Each individual's soul is made up of a different set of pieces, some older, some younger. The pieces go through many cycles, in different combinations, always getting polished, until each becomes as bright and clear as glass, after which it joins with the soul of a queen, destined to live forever."

Saxon found himself smiling at the image. "That's lovely," he said softly. "I believe that because there's the chance that my people are wrong about the afterlife, I need to do everything that I can while I'm alive, to leave a legacy that's worthy."

He could feel the others withdraw slightly. Or perhaps that was just his imagination.

"What if staying alive no longer feels right?" Gawain asked after a few moments.

"When faced with a great enemy, and the chance to have a death that is worthy, that means something? Then it's called being heroic," Saxon said. "If you're struggling with the pain of living day to day, there are people who can help."

Or at least he hoped they could help. He didn't know of any therapies that might work on a Chonchu. And while Basil was good, what sort of antidepressants did one use on a ship?

The sigh that followed was worthy of Eleanor at her most expressive.

"Talk to me," Saxon said. Hopefully they could get the ship's engines past this. At least get them safely out of the current hyperspace tunnel.

"Tell us of your grief," Gawain said in reply.

"I see," Saxon said. He swallowed hard, looking down at the black skin of his palms, the white fur of his wrists. "It's as stark as this contrast," he said slowly, drawing a sharp talon from the white to the dark. "One minute, the world is happy. You may have some knots in your fur, but they can be teased out, or even clipped away by your mates. Then, the darkness hits."

Saxon shuddered. "You can no longer see your path. Your footing becomes as treacherous as a melting ice flow. Your life hangs on a single thread. One tiny slip, and the darkness will take you."

He paused, then made himself continue. "My brother was my connection to my family. As well as the continuation of it, with my nieces and nephews. But Maxwell is gone. That bright light snuffed out. My sister hasn't forbidden contact, hasn't declared me an outlaw. She isn't encouraging me to come back, either. Instead of a simple line between myself and my clan, the way is cloudy, covered with ice. It will never be easy to connect to them again. It will always be different, difficult. Always cold. I've lost that part that I never realized I relied on. That I considered central to my identity. My clan is gone, and I'll never recover them."

That was truly what Maxwell's death had meant to Saxon, though he hadn't been able to express it to himself that way before now.

"No matter how much money or goods or gifts I may be able to snow down on my clan in the future, Flora will never willingly accept me again."

Saxon knew the type of stubbornness he saw in his sister. It might be one of the things he recognized in Judit. He, himself, wasn't necessarily as stubborn. He was more willing to give way about things.

Not Flora.

"But you will try anyway?" Gawain now asked. "Try to reconnect with your clan? Your people?"

"I will," Saxon said. "There is no glory in dying without trying." His people didn't frown on suicide, but it was always supposed to have a meaning. Not some silly teenager mooning over another. People had committed public suicide to protest throughout the years, as a way of drawing attention to serious issues. It was still an accepted form of death.

The silence grew long. Were Gawain and Abban talking to each other? Talking with Eleanor?

"We will try," Abban said after a few moments.

"But still…we want to go home," Gawain added.

"I'll talk with the others," Saxon promised.

He shook his head as he rose from his chair, feeling as though he were shedding cobwebs and dust.

He'd been wanting someone to call on him to do something.

Saving the ship was worth rejoining the living.

CHAPTER 24

JUDIT

"Jᴛᴀᴅᴛ?"

"Hmmm?" Judit said, looking up from her tablet. Damn it! She was just starting to really lose herself in this novel.

But duty called.

"Yes, Eleanor, what is it?" Judit asked after a few moments.

She was sitting in the comfy chair of her office. The ship was currently attached to the *Frieze* space station. It was a smaller station and not one that had been built all at once, but had grown more organically, so it looked like a series of shipping containers that had been welding together.

Who knew? That might have been the origin of the station, and whoever was in charge had just kept up the motif.

She wouldn't say that it was a smuggler's haven, *per se*. However, she was fairly certain that a large percentage of the goods that passed through this station weren't legal in many systems, or that whatever bills of lading were being presented didn't remotely match what was actually in the cargo holds.

They'd come here hoping that Menefry might still find

them a cloaking device, since Dale had shipped off the *Balmor* system. He'd left some additional material and wires as well as a few extra controllers, but that wasn't enough. Given time and unlimited funds, Basil thought that zie could build a specialized 3D printer that would produce the wires that Dale had. But nothing they had on the ship would do it. Plus, it would call for even more exotic chemicals than Basil had on hand.

So they were back to square one with that.

Judit's window faced away from the station, which meant she got to watch all the cargo ships coming and going. She wasn't surprised that there was so much traffic. Again, most of it probably wasn't legal.

What sorts of bribes did the station pay to the Cartel, to keep the hypergates open? Were they raided occasionally? Judit had never knowingly carried contraband. She'd always figured that was a sure-fire way to lose her license.

Now, she wasn't so sure. Maybe she needed to expand her idea of legitimate cargo. Those runs, while tricky, were also much more lucrative.

"You said that I should come to you if there was a problem," Eleanor said.

Judit put her tablet on the small table beside her, picking up her coffee mug instead. It was still warm and slightly bitter, just how she liked it. "Yes, you should," Judit said. "What is it?"

She'd heard from Saxon about Gawain and Abban, and their talk during the last hyperspace run on the way to the *Frieze* station. She should have expected that Eleanor would come and talk with her sooner rather than later.

"I'm worried," Eleanor said.

"About?" Judit prompted.

When she was met with more silence, she added, "Gawain and Abban? The ship? The crew?"

"Me."

"Oh, *édesem*," Judit said. She wished there was a way that she could physically hug the other being. Eleanor sounded like she was six years old, all alone and afraid of the dark.

Or at the very least, knock the heads of Gawain and Abban together and bash some sense into them.

"The boys are still being difficult?" Judit said.

There was that expressive sigh. "Yes," Eleanor said. "And I can't stand it. I just…I can't be this alone. It isn't fair."

"No, it isn't," Judit said. She gave her own sigh, quieter than Eleanor's, and tinged with much more sadness. "What do you need for us to do?"

"I don't know," Eleanor said.

Judit couldn't help it. She snorted. "You know exactly what you'd like for us to do. You're just afraid you can't ask for it."

"If you were Chonchu, I might approach the others about the *Jaimeng*, the joining. It's when an individual of one pod feels more alive with the members of a different pod. It's a simple ritual to change one's alliance, to move from one pod to another. However, it has profound repercussions and is never approached lightly. But you…I think you would fit well with me. With us."

Eleanor sighed again. "And I *never* used to do that. To just think about myself. It took so much work at the beginning to say 'I' and 'me' and now I say those automatically. The others are *other* to me. They hide things from me. I can't stand it. I'm so alone."

The last few words were rendered in a heartbreaking wail. Judit's entire soul ached just listening to the grief in the other person's voice.

"We need to go back to the Chonchu system, don't we?" Judit said after a few moments, giving her companion the time to recompose herself.

"I'm afraid to go back," Eleanor admitted. "I'm afraid of what will happen to us. But I'm more afraid of what will happen if we don't."

"I'll call a meeting with the others," Judit said. "They have to have a vote in whether or not they stay on the ship or if they need to get off here."

"I see," Eleanor said, sounding hesitant. "All right. Let them vote. But…"

"But what?" Judit asked, dread filling her.

"But it needs to be soon."

"I'll make it happen," Judit said.

"Thank you," Eleanor said.

An audible click echoed through the office and Judit knew that she was alone again.

She would call the rest of the crew to gather shortly.

But first, she had to talk with Basil.

CHAPTER 25

BASIL

Basil stood outside Judit's office door. It was closed, but the green light was on, so zie knew that zie was expected.

Zie still hesitated.

Nothing that zie had done the last half day had felt right. Zie kept telling zieself that it was the right thing to do, the smart thing to do. They were facing too many unknowns.

It still didn't sit well in zir segments. And zie was afraid that eventually zie would never be able to wash off that stink.

Still, zie made zieself grow and arm, reach up, and knock on Judit's door.

It took a few moments before the door opened. She had probably been sitting in her other chair, looking out the window, instead of sitting at her desk.

"Come in," Judit said, gesturing for Basil to enter.

The office was the same as it ever was. Clean. Neat. A few odd books scattered to the side of the gray expanse of a desk, a couple of different tablets. Incongruously, a small wooden flower, painted brilliant red—a tulip, the national flower of Hungary—stood to one side. The walls were still painted different colors, green and blue, which Basil found oddly soothing.

Judit didn't say anything until after Basil had come to rest in front of the desk and the door had shut behind zim.

"How successful were you?" she asked, her tone sharp.

Basil tilted zir head from side to side. "I re-installed as many of the 'leashes' as I could. You should be able to override all the automated flying modules from the main helm. Also, all life support and gravity is now routed through the main helm."

Judit nodded slowly. "Is it enough?"

Basil found zieself giving a barking laugh. It wasn't hysterical, though zie could hear the tinges of sheer recklessness around the edges of it.

"Who knows?" zie said. Zie shook zir head, unfocusing zir sensing array for a few moments. "The systems are designed to grow together. The ship is still mechanical for the most part. But…" zie hesitated.

"But?" Judit prompted.

"I found additional stubs of wires growing in some of the conduit tubes," Basil said all in a rush. "Biological wires, like what I see in the secondary engine room."

"So Eleanor may have more control over the entire ship than we originally believed?" Judit asked.

"Yes," Basil said. "I think…I think she's in the process of *becoming* the ship. Of taking over all the parts of it. Slowly."

"Was this part of the original plan?" Judit asked. "Something that Masala never got around to telling us about?"

"I'm not sure about that," Basil said. "Remember when I had to find new nutrients to feed the engines, so that they could regrow the part of the secondary engine that I'd removed?"

"Yes," Judit said, nodding.

"I think that may have also been the impetus for the

additional growth and spread of the biological wires," Basil said.

"So they haven't been growing for very long."

"No, but they do grow quickly."

Judit tilted her head to one side. Basil could see the computations that appeared to be running behind her eyes.

"I wonder—was it Eleanor who started growing such structures? Or one of the others?"

Basil felt zir segments stiffen in surprise. Zie hadn't even considered that.

Judit continued with her musings. "Are they planning on taking over? Completely freezing Eleanor out? And us, as well?"

"I don't know," Basil said.

Judit nodded. "We'll ask them later. For now, we have a meeting to get to. A decision to make."

Basil held up zir one hand to get Judit to pause. "I will vote to stay with the ship. Even if it means dying in a ball of fiery glory."

Judit snorted. "I have no intention of dying, either in fire or in glory," she said. "It's time. We need to go talk with the others. See if we can get a consensus about our next step."

Basil slid zir tail to the side, then inched out of the way, out the door of Judit's office.

It was time for a decision, to see which of the crew would stay.

And who would go.

CHAPTER 26

SAXON

Saxon stood in the winter conference room, waiting for the others.

Originally, the meeting had been scheduled for the woods room, which was where they generally met.

However, Gawain of all people had been the one to suggest meeting in here instead.

It was the room that Saxon was the most comfortable in. The holograms portrayed the sky across the ceiling as an incredible, searing blue. Drifts of snow surrounded them on all sides, with a clear path out one direction, a trail leading off into the distance and vanishing at the horizon. He could almost feel the cool winds ruffling his fur. Occasionally, the sound of sifting snow wafted through the air. The smell of metal and frozen rocks called to him.

Home.

He understood that not everyone liked this room. Judit had grown quite fond of it, and had sometimes met there with Saxon, particularly when they'd decided to play cards together, drink something alcoholic, and insult each other's relatives with curses in their own native languages. He'd also seen Kim in here, though her visiting was for a different purpose. It appeared that disappearing against a snow bank was actually difficult, particularly for a perfectionist such as herself. There were multiple layers of shade to work with, and snow really wasn't a single color. It had been fascinating watching her fade into the background, and surprising when she'd reappeared much closer to the door. He hadn't seen her move.

Something changed. Saxon wasn't sure what. It hadn't been an audible noise. But he suddenly knew that he was no longer alone.

When he turned, he saw that a hologram had appeared in the center of the conference table. He was used to seeing the single amber spar that represented Eleanor. He wasn't surprised to see three spars this time, one for each of the three people who made up the ship's secondary engines.

"Hello Eleanor, Gawain, Abban," Saxon said gravely, nodding his head toward each.

"Hello, Saxon!" Abban said. Zie actually sounded excited, which was unusual. Normally, the digger was the most laid-back about things.

"How are you, Abban?" Saxon said, turning his full attention onto the shortest of the three spars. He'd been meeting regularly with both Gawain and Abban, feeling their way toward a friendship.

"Very good," Abban said. Zie continued to sound more chipper than usual. Was zie also talking to Kim occasionally? "This is an important meeting today."

"Yes, it is," Saxon said. He knew that it was something of a foregone conclusion: the three Chonchu needed to go back to their home system, to be back in the presence of one of their queens.

This meeting was more to decide who would stay on the ship, and who would bail.

"We hope—we hope to be able to show you our home," Abban said after a few moments.

Saxon couldn't help but smile. "I would like that," he said gravely.

He knew that there were no guarantees that he, or anyone on the ship, would survive such an encounter.

Was it worth the risk?

Before he could say anything else, Kim came bopping in. "Hi there!" she said. "Hi Gawain, Abban, Eleanor," she said cheerily as she sat down on her chair.

"Hello, Kim," Gawain said. He asked something in Kim's native Bantel language that made her crack up.

"That's a good one, Gawain!" Kim said.

Saxon was curious about their relationship, but really, it was none of his business.

Menefry came in next. He bowed his head slightly to the three individuals on the table before taking his kneeling chair. He looked around the room and couldn't hide his shudder.

Saxon managed to not roll his eyes. Yes, this room wasn't as comfortable as the desert room. But they wouldn't be there for too long. As he went to his own chair, Judit and Basil came in, together. It wouldn't surprise Saxon if they'd been meeting before the meeting.

Judit walked around to the front of the table. "Hello, everyone," she said. "I'm glad to see we're all here."

Menefry raised one of his weight-bearing arms, like he was in a class and had a question.

Judit appeared to be expecting it, though, because she just nodded at him as she took her chair.

Menefry sang out in a clear voice, obviously a blessing or prayer for this occasion.

Saxon raised his head, as he'd been taught to do as a child, eyes wide open, staring at the blue sky overhead. He felt his heart settle more in his chest as he breathed in the cold, accepting his fate.

By the time Menefry finished, Saxon knew his choice.

———

Judit laid out the problem succinctly: the three beings who made up the ship's secondary engine needed to go back to the Chonchu system.

"So let's go!" Kim had chirped.

"Not so fast," Judit said. "We don't know what will happen when Eleanor, Gawain, and Abban are back under the influence of the queens."

"Oh," Kim said, deflating.

"What do you think will happen?" Eleanor inquired. She sounded puzzled.

"Will you maintain your individualism?" Basil asked. "Or will the queens completely absorb you? Will you still be able to fly the ship? Or will you be overwhelmed?"

"The queens won't hurt us," Gawain said, sounding horrified.

"How do you know?" Saxon shot back. "You are different, now. More individual. Will the queens allow you to continue to exist?"

"We think so," Eleanor said quietly. "But you needn't worry about yourselves. The queens won't harm you."

"Will they realize that there are other people on the ship? Or will they just see you?" Judit asked. "Will they crash the ship? Remember, according to you, it was part of the reason why Masala installed so many 'leashes' on you in the first place. In case you came back in touch with the hive mind and lost yourselves."

Abban gave zir harsh laugh, "Ha! Ha!" Zie had still not really learned how to laugh, though zie did find more things funny than zie used to. Zie tended to be very literal about everything. "You are safe. Will be safe."

"There's no way of knowing that for certain, though," Gawain suddenly broke in. "However, I also believe that you will all be safe."

Saxon nodded. He'd already decided to risk it all. Hearing that the three Chonchu believed they wouldn't be instantly killed did make that decision weigh easier against his fur.

"You do understand that all we've ever heard about the queens is propaganda from the Cartel," Saxon said. "We, or at least Arthur, was convinced that was a bunch of hooey."

"Like what?" Eleanor asked.

"That the queens were power hungry. That as a hive mind, they were a risk to all individuals. That they could somehow take over everyone," Basil said.

"Oh, dear," Eleanor said.

Quiet filled the room. Saxon could hear the sifting of the snow. But which way was the wind now blowing?

"You understand that all the queens want, all they've ever wanted, was universal harmony? They thought it was a sign that the Cartel was named Universal?" Eleanor said after a few moments. "It was why they welcomed the aliens, gave them so much access at the beginning."

"I saw footage of one queen's group of warriors attacking another," Saxon said. He had remembered that recording vividly, as it showed a general lack of tactics on both sides. They just appeared to want to overwhelm each other.

"That was a historic recreation," Gawain said. "It wasn't real."

"So the queens aren't continually fighting one another? Trying to gain more power, more influence?" Menefry said. He sounded thoughtful.

"When the queens were younger, yes. Of course they

were. But they discovered that mutual cooperation was a much better way to survive and to grow the species," Eleanor replied. "That was why they were working with Arthur. So that they could continue to grow the species. They won't destroy their prodigy out of hand."

"I think we need to take a vote," Judit said. "Nothing binding. But a place holder, where are we are at this time." She paused before continuing in a more formal tone. "Who chooses to go with the ship to the Chonchu system, understanding that it may be dangerous, possibly deadly?"

"I'll go," Menefry said. "The Goddess has plans for your queens. I'm sure of it."

"Kim?" Judit asked, obviously going around the table.

"We have a bunch of working escape pods, right?" Kim asked, looking from side to side for confirmation.

"Yes. Ten," Basil said. "Two for each of the base crew."

"Then let's go for it! I say we rewire what's necessary so that we can operate the ship from the escape pods, if it comes to that," Kim said.

Saxon found himself nodding. That was actually a very interesting idea. He wasn't sure how feasible it was.

Basil was next. "I'm in," zie said. "I want to meet with your scientists, see if I can't improve your systems more."

"I'm also game," Saxon said. He didn't add, *What was the worst that could happen?* Because he knew that included the ship imploding and them all dying in a horrible fireball.

"And I," Judit said, "would be happy to pilot you all there. Abban? Gawain? Eleanor? What say you?"

"Yes, let's return to the home world," Eleanor replied first.

"Yes! Yes! Yes!" Abban said gleefully.

"I concur," Gawain said, his deep voice sounding formal.

"Then let us return to the place of Universal Harmony," Judit said. "And hope that doesn't get us all killed."

EPILOGUE

CLAYTON

Clayton wandered into Fredrick's office late that night, after he was certain that the Yu'udir had already headed back to his apartment or rooms or wherever he was staying. Clayton had only been here once or twice.

The walls were covered in screens, but not so that Fredrick could surround himself in holograms of ice and snow. When Clayton flicked on a screen, all it showed was a constant stream of numbers and words.

Clayton understood the Yu'udir's obsession with data. He had the same inclinations, to surround himself with it, absorb it, drink it in.

But then Clayton would turn around and use the data. Whereas the Yu'udir appeared to just…wallow in it.

Clayton stepped further into the room. He didn't bother controlling his shudder. It was such a small space! Just over two meters on a side. How did the overly large Yu'udir stand it? Desks lined each wall, under the screens. The projector hung in the middle of the ceiling, ready to display even more data. The air smelled stale despite how cool the room felt.

On the far side of Fredrick's desk, tucked in between two

screens, hung a sticky-board. Any paper you slapped on it was automatically attached and would hang there until you peeled it off.

That was what Clayton was looking for, though he didn't know it until he saw it.

That picture of a Bantel, with sad eyes, wearing Universal blue.

Had she been attracted to Fredrick? Something personal?

No, this was the Bantel who'd killed herself. Clayton remembered the name. Riley. Fredrick hadn't mentioned her in any of his reports, but Clayton had seen the request to get her transferred to his team.

Fredrick's reaction to her death had been enlightening.

Clayton hadn't needed his opinion of the Yu'udir confirmed—that Fredrick lacked that killing instinct. But this Riley's death had absolutely made it clear that Fredrick wasn't cut out for this type of work.

Clayton didn't want to let Fredrick go, though. Not because of some stupid sentimentality. Clayton never indulged in that sort of nonsense. Fredrick really did have good instincts when it came to tracking down those hidden vessels, the ones with the phony registrations.

He was going to have to ease Fredrick out of the rest of his affairs, though. Retire that good hunting dog. He'd just expected more, and while the results that Fredrick had come up with were good, they weren't good enough to justify the expense.

Clayton turned to leave the office, but something made him pause and pull Riley's badge picture up off of Fredrick's board, looking on the back of it.

The company name listed there gave Clayton chills.

It was the name of one of the four companies that Clayton's shell companies had paid out an extraordinary amount of credits to recently.

One of the companies owned by Sachiko.

What did it mean? How had Fredrick linked Sachiko to Riley? And all that Sachiko implied?

Shaken, Clayton let the picture fall onto the desk as he stumbled away.

Was his hunting dog really tame?

Or had Fredrick found a new scent that he was pursuing, and not bothering to tell his master about?

Clayton was going to have to watch Fredrick very, *very* carefully from now on.

And then…well, Clayton had no compunction over ending a competitor's life.

Or even a close working colleague.

READ MORE!

Be sure to pick up all the books in the Long Run series.

Project Nemesis
Project Nyx
Project Tisiphone
Project Persephone

Available at your favorite retailers!

ABOUT THE AUTHOR

Leah Cutter writes page-turning fiction in exotic locations, such as a magical New Orleans, the ancient Orient, Hungary, the Oregon coast, rural Kentucky, Seattle, Minneapolis, and many others.

She writes literary, fantasy, mystery, science fiction, and horror fiction. Her short fiction has been published in magazines like *Alfred Hitchcock's Mystery Magazine* and *Talebones*, anthologies like Fiction River, and on the web. Her long fiction has been published both by New York publishers as well as small presses.

Find Leah's books on Knotted Road Press at (www.KnottedRoadPress.com)

Follow her blog at www.LeahCutter.com.

Reviews

It's true. Reviews help me sell more books. If you've enjoyed this story, please consider leaving a review of it on your favorite site.

Come someplace new...

Are you a traveler? Do you enjoy exploring strange new worlds, new cultures, new people?

Journey into the various lands envisioned by Leah Cutter.

Sign up for my newsletter and I'll start you on your travels with a free copy of my book, *The Island Sampler*.

I will never spam you or use your email for nefarious purposes. You can also unsubscribe at any time.

http://www.LeahCutter.com/newsletter/

ABOUT KNOTTED ROAD PRESS

Knotted Road Press fiction specializes in dynamic writing set in mysterious, exotic locations.

Knotted Road Press non-fiction publishes autobiographies, business books, cookbooks, and how-to books with unique voices.

Knotted Road Press creates DRM-free ebooks as well as high-quality print books for readers around the world.

With authors in a variety of genres including literary, poetry, mystery, fantasy, and science fiction, Knotted Road Press has something for everyone.

Knotted Road Press
www.KnottedRoadPress.com